Some Like It Intense

Samar Demir

Title: Some Like It Intense
Author: Samar Demir
Illustrator: Shirin Malekesmaili

ISBN: 9798831828061
ISBN: 9781739660321
eISBN: 9781739660390

Firouz Media Limited
www.firouzmedia.com
IG: @firouzmedia

PROLOGUE

When my therapist asked me about the concept of love, I moved away from her and her fleeting gaze and trailed fingers along her walls. I could feel her hands twirling her pen and the rhythmic way she held her breath but there was so much hidden underneath the words; things that I couldn't quite put into words. The lighting in her office was low, and the curtains closed but when I peered deeper, I could still see the outline of a sun. How long had it been since I stepped in? I couldn't tell but I could safely guess it had been over thirty minutes. There wasn't anything to say. Just as quickly as she said those words, the silence crept in so that what was left was an infinite amount of awkward silence. She called my name again and I heard her voice as a throaty surrender. My name on her lips felt like a mouthful as if she had said it ten thousand times over and was getting a little bit tired of saying it. "Say something," she whispered. "What do you think love is?" I turned around to meet her gaze.

For a second, I thought she looked like me: cold and afraid of the world. When I looked again, I saw that she was different and stable and I was not. That realization burnt holes in the back of my neck. She looked at me, lips pursed, daring me to speak. I wanted to tell her about the men I'd loved in my lifetime and how I'd given each one a part of me I couldn't have back. I wanted her to know about the purple sunlight and the insecurities a woman like me had faced in the receding lights of fireworks. I wanted to tell her that love comes and it goes and that there was no other way to it.

Instead, I glanced away.

CHAPTER ONE
Autumn Man

I was but a young child when I first discovered that change happened ever so often and dreams barely lasted the night. Of course, this fact came about as I spent my early years growing into a family that did not love me. I did not know love in its forgiving form but I knew that it felt like coming up for air after being submerged in waters for so long. Most of the time, I had my life and future all planned out. I wasn't the sort of girl who lived in the present simply as a warning for the past. I ached for the future in the way the sun would beat in a carnivorous pattern, escaping the clutches of my tired fingers.

As I grew up, I often would find myself wandering around the streets, clutching my purse and thinking. What would life be if I had just a little bit of adventure? I lived in Istanbul, Turkey, and had a simple enough life. There wasn't much mystery in Istanbul where I grew up. I knew the brittle song of the morning bird by heart and could touch the sun with both hands. It wasn't much up for thinking because I knew the people who walked down the streets in search of a basket of nothing. I was twenty-eight, almost happy, and almost satisfied with my life in the city. Not so in love with the city, but comfortable enough to call it home. Home, to me, was not measured in calculated stares or the defiant smiles of unhappy people. The home was simply a place good enough to live and die in. And Istanbul proved time and again to be just that for me. I was twenty-eight years old when the idea of a family struck again and one day when I curled up underneath the sheets in my apartment, I thought about my mother and my father and the kitchen sink and how each morning, I'd find it colored red with their arguments. When the people I call my friends asked me about my family, I told them I had one before. I truly did. That memory floated about for a year and a half and then it was gone. Once, before I'd left home, I screamed at my mother, asked her why couldn't she love me like a normal person.

She screamed back, "Tell me it isn't love when I pushed you out of my womb." She did not cry. When she said that, all I thought about was the sacred difference between love that is obligatory and love that is given openly, with both hands. I knew I couldn't stay once I had my fill of love that wasn't right.

People think that I do not quickly give up on love. Perhaps they are not totally wrong. I've always wanted the right kind of love but I've also been too uptight to want it with the whole of my heart. I've pushed people away for the fun of it whilst still harboring thoughts of falling in love.

Istanbul wasn't the city to live in if you were like me. I loved adventure. I loved freedom. I loved privacy, and I didn't really get all of that in the city. All I got was a job in a publishing firm and an emptiness that felt dragged. No, the pay was good, and that was the problem. The publishing firm afforded me the chance to be constantly creative. It was the one thing that helped in pushing me off my bed in the mornings. Before this illustrating job, I had worked in a bookstore, stacking books and dusting the shelves, and pretending I was one with the universe strung up in my head. The people who'd walked in to buy the books would look at me with chemical eyes; the sort one would do to a stranger they'd never see again and I would understand the fluency in their setting silence. At the publishing firm, everything felt right. Granted the mystery was not as I ached for but it was something and each morning, as I prepared for work, I'd look at myself in the mirror and reimagine a lifetime of secret lives tucked away in a haven.

Two years before I'd moved away from home, I got the job. On my first day, my mother walked into the living room. From the corners of my eyes, I saw her. She looked like she was tired of a thousand different things all at once but she needed to say something. It was all obligatory, and mandatory for a mother to ask her child about work. Our relationship never evolved more than those clear-cut differences and I was fairly certain it never would. I saw her lean against the doorframe, her breath heavy.

Are you happy?

Her question had struck me as odd. She could have asked about work but instead, she'd asked something most unexpected.

"I am," I told her.

She swallowed. We both knew it was a lie. My little sister walked in on us and tucked one strand of hair behind her ears. My mother told her to go wear a hijab but when my sister looked at me, I could tell she'd grow to despise this life too and how each heated conversation would invariably drive her out just like it did me. On my first and second days at work, I quickly came to enjoy the atmosphere. The people who worked with me did not pay much attention and for a while, the silence was the most beautiful thing I ever came to know.

When I met him, I called him the Autumn man. It wasn't his real name. His real name was something Turkish but because of his looks and the way he reminded me of autumn, I gave him the name. His wild eyes and his playful gaze first caught my attention and when he walked, I watched him, teasingly, throbbing inwardly for him to look at me too. He floated about. That's what I called it: floating. He was never in one place at a time and it was a mystery in every form. We were opposites. While he had a mass of dark hair with streaks of gray on his head, mine was a golden brown, piled atop my head in a messy bun. I usually cover mine with a scarf but his was as wild as the ocean. It was his eyes that first caught me off-guard. They were maybe almost blue but it reminded me of the skylines and it would not go away. He was mysterious and for some reason, I slowly fell in love with Autumn man.

The first time we talked, I found that he had a soft voice, almost like a whisper, and a smile that resembled longing. We did not talk about the weather or how my table had a dying plant. We simply talked about the economy and the government. He asked about what I considered a good enough topics to write on and I hesitated because no one had ever asked me that in the delicate way his voice had formed the words. I was desperately in need of someone I could lean on and Autumn man looked like the sort of person I could do that with. Of course, we did not start as a budding relationship. In fact, all we had for the following weeks was a meeting edged between works and writing and editing. There was nothing else even though I wanted for there to be. This man did not want to be in a relationship. He'd said so himself on one of our work-related discussions. Yet as we began to welcome the idea of communication that surpassed both our expectations, the need arose again. I did not dare to walk up to him about my feelings. When Autumn man told me he thought I was pretty with the red lipstick, I went home and I got myself a box of red lipsticks. It was funny how quickly his want for some things affected mine too but it was this feeling that drove me down into the way I handled things.

The feeling was not as it was; not demanding or quick. It was more a necessity at first; like a budding need to remove the longing in my heart but one day, he offered to walk me to the bus. It was raining and he had an umbrella and as we walked, he said,

"Do you maybe want to date me?"

Later I would tell myself his question had invoked within me the sort of knowledge that drove mere men insane. I was filled with more longing, sure, but there was something more. When we kissed, a week later in my apartment, I threw away the confines of the teachings my mother had taught me, and my sister and I let him trail his fingers along my skin like a painting.

Autumn man could easily have passed as a guardian. He was much older than me and had seen enough of life to know where to kiss and where to touch. The relationship was not complicated because I'd fallen in love with him long before that question had fallen from his lips in a hurry. There were times, however, wherein I had wanted some sort of complication. I did not tell my mother. We'd become estranged during that time and the thought of speaking to her did not in any way appease me. The man that I was in love with reminded me of a sad painting, one I could touch and admire and ache for. He would provide me with safety and attention and I would bend and break for him. We flowed in that pattern; in that rhythmic way of hand touching and breathless loving. It wasn't long after that I found a fault in him, a fault that I couldn't quite let go of.

I discovered that Autumn man did not love me. Well, he did, sometimes but not often. All my life I had always yearned for love but Autumn man told me one night he could not love me. We were in my apartment lying about in an armchair when he blurted out the words.

I moved away from him. "Don't tell me that, please."

He glanced past my head and away at the silvery moon halved by my curtains. Then, when he looked at me, a part of my soul warned me, told me to run but I did not. The love within my heart was much too powerful and real to let go of. I would permanently ignore that red flag, sort of, and help him learn how to love me completely.

He said, —"Teach me, Fidan..." —He wasn't born in Turkey and his Turkish wasn't perfect so he leaned cleverly into English. —"I will teach you," I whispered to him. —"Hold my hands."

I learned once, that love was fleeting in every sense and that one only needed to know that to be free. Yet freedom was born into my very being, twisting and turning with remarkable ease. I was free with this man and with this freedom came the belonging. Autumn man was a person to be reckoned with. I was not attracted to his money although he had enough to spare. The tradition of things I'd always known was for my husband to be kind and helpful and to provide me with money so that I would not lack things. It was true. I expected that from Autumn man because we were in a relationship and he seemed to need to become one with me. We did not necessarily talk about that, though, but within the confines of old conversations, it was evident. He would marry me someday and everything would be right forever.

I knew also that I would not marry him because of his self-sacrifice and kindness, because I was neither devoted nor kind, and I could not accept what I could not compensate for. I would marry him because of his intelligence. Not for his brain, but for a very complex and intricate arrangement of dimly lit spaces. It was for his intelligence - or rather, his intellect, and his progressive body of consciousness, his rich intelligence, his unquestioning dominance over facts, theories, and data that I fell for him. My eyes, first of all, searched his gaze. His gaze was the same intelligence that I relied on. And I knew, very well, that he was the one.

My life was not as intricately placed as his. Mine was pretty simple, the habits old. His was layered as if the very idea of being simple did not appeal to his lifestyle. Before we began seeing, I'd always considered myself to be old-fashioned but safely aware that I needed change. Autumn man was not the change I sought but he fit into it perfectly. I watched him in the little things that he did and how each turn had been comical, almost, to watch. We did not go out together in public for the starting part of the relationship. He did not voice it but I could tell there would be something terrible in us being seen together in a relationship. My mother called after work. I was in the shower when I heard the phone ringing. I wanted to ignore it but I also didn't want to miss Autumn man's calls. We'd agreed on meeting tonight in my apartment. I hadn't ever seen his, however, but often, the thought never crossed my mind.

When I stepped out of the shower, I saw it was my mother. We hadn't talked in a while and suddenly I saw her name scrawled across the front screen. I hesitated. This moment brought with it some measure of nostalgia. I pushed the hair behind my ears and leaned over so that water dripped from my body and unto the wooden table which held both my lava lamp and my phone.

The call ended before the music ended. I waited only about five seconds before she called again. This time, I took the call.

"Good morning, mother," I said to her in Turkish.

It was a good thing I'd brushed up my skills because even though ninety-nine percent of people in Istanbul spoke Turkish, a good number, like Autumn man, used English. With him, I wasn't worried about forgetting how to speak. He was a true talker but he let me speak. She hesitated as if regretting her fragile hands touching her phone and finding my number.

For a while, the silence remained like an absorbing detail and it flowed between my fingers and my slow intake of breaths. I could already picture her outside on the balcony, her shawl held tightly in place by her years of knowing how to wrap one.

"How are you, Fidan?" she asked. Her voice was unusually low but I took it for what it was: a silent plea. "I am fine," I said to her.

We waited —mother and daughter— for one of us to say something but there was nothing. I, for one, did not want to be the person easing into a conversation with her. We'd since passed the episode of dutifully talking or asking after the other. In truth, I did not consider her to be anything close to an emotional attachment and I could guess she felt the same way too. Then, suddenly, her voice broke through the barriers. "When are you going to visit home?"

Home? I wanted to ask her what she felt the home was but my voice would not come out. She had never asked me that before nor intended for me to call it home but now she was asking me a question I couldn't quite answer.

"Did you hear me, Fidan?" she asked.
I sighed. "Maybe tomorrow, Ma."
We both knew I was telling a lie.

"Okay, then. I'll make your favorite: Köfte."

I laughed. Köfte was no longer a favorite but, if course, she couldn't know that. She didn't know I'd changed and, yes, I couldn't blame her. I barely knew I had changed too. With Autumn man, these changes were never evident but alone, with my mother and her heavy accent, it was. Almost.

"Look, ma, I've got...to go now." I could see her nodding. "Okay, okay. Maybe tomorrow then."

After she hung up, I tiptoed to my room, placed the phone against a pillow and pulled open my wardrobe. It was evening and the moon was out and the stars glistened against my curtains. I wanted to select something cool and light, something

Autumn man would love but as my eyes scanned for clothes, I caught the wisps of a second change. My choice of clothes when I was him was not reserved. It was always bright and skimpy and showed my skin in places I used to preserve. With him, I was never ashamed or afraid of being seen or felt or touched. He excited me because he was mysterious and strong and stable and he was all I had ever wanted in my life as a woman living in Istanbul and working in a publishing firm as an illustrator.

I got dressed in a red gown and proceeded to the kitchen to boil rice. Autumn man loved rice, said it smelt like a thousand different sunrises and I liked how poetic he was with his emotions and the things he usually liked. First, I poured the rice in a bowl. I needed to get all the dirt out. Then I put it in a pot and turned on the stove. For a little while I watched the flames dance dizzily against the edge and I fancied the audacity of the blue and orange flames, naked against the pot. I poured in water and closed the pot. It was my mother who'd showed me how to cook. My first attempt had been too bad so that when her hands grazed the sides of my cheeks, I knew I had to be better. And I was. I really was. When the water began boiling, I turned off the stove, poured the water away and added in a bit of salt. It was at this time that my phone rang again. I did not check the caller ID immediately. It could still be my mother, I thought, with a selfish groan. When I checked, Autumn man's name was on the screen.

I took the call with a shy smile. Couldn't he tell

that I was more than excited?

His voice was cold and calculating and it was what I thought about as I sank deeper into the web of the conversation.
"I won't come tonight, Fidan," he said.

I waited for an explanation but there was none. He wasn't drawing his breath. He was done with the conversation. It let me think: Did I do something wrong or was this some sort of trick? I couldn't tell. I couldn't guess. I simply needed to know. "I don't understand," I whispered. In my defense, I didn't know my voice had become sort of a whisper. I knew I was fidgeting with my hair and the rice was boiling on the stove and the moon was out and the stars were beautiful. I knew those things like a second skin. And yet I did not know that I was laced with an animalistic panic; one that was tearing at my skin and unbecoming of a woman like me. He said —and this time his voice was colder— "I have got so much to do. Work and meetings and everything, you know."

When he said those things, I immediately thought about my sister and how, in those early years, she'd looked up to me with wondering eyes. I remembered, once, when we ran down to a neighbor's pool. The poor neighbors had traveled and I was sixteen and angry at nothing in particular. My sister and I did not take off our hijabs because we couldn't but we flung ourselves into the pool and she almost drowned. I remembered the fear as I pulled her out; how her body had felt so weak and unrealistic as I called out for her. It was this feeling which now clawed at my chest as I listened to my lover. By this time, we'd been dating for a year and a half.

"I've got work too," I said to him. I was angry and maybe I was right to. "But I figured we needed to take a break from it all and be happy."

He did not hesitate and I did not expect him to. "I can't —not tonight. I'll make it up to you." There was a strain in his voice, a moment of weakness where I did not know him and he did not know me. I pressed the phone closer to my ears, afraid that if I let it go, it would be the end of us. I didn't want that. I wanted everything with him. Autumn man had made countless promises with me and I was unwilling to let it all go.

"Can you hear me, Fidan?" he asked. I sniffed and wasn't aware that I'd been crying. It was hard to understand a lot of things with the world pressing heavily against my throat.

"I can," I replied. "I made rice."

He said nothing but I could hear a fan whirring in the background, and just faintly, the sounds of moving cars. First, love comes and then awareness, like now. I was aware of a thousand different things as I stood in the kitchen in this reckless body of mine. The problem with this kind of awareness was that it came as suddenly and left with it a sour taste. It was new everytime. And their collection did not lead me to a lasting and useful knowledge forever.

This might seem like it, but in fact, I have learned that applying the teachings of love in the past to a newly formed romantic relationship is the surest way to ruin it. I had a lot of questions in my head. I wanted to pour them all on one body. I wanted immediate answers. I had not experienced love before him. But heck, I don't think there was love in him. I was afraid of love and intimacy before him. Still there was that hunger and eagerness to have all of it with him. I needed to be loved, to feel that power within me and all of a sudden, it was all gone, replaced by a feverish ache.

"Do you see a future with me, A?" I asked suddenly.
" Fidan —"
"Just answer the question, please."

He hesitated. I knew Autumn man. He never hesitated and yet in this very moment, he did and it broke my heart. I hung up, switched off my phone and turned off the stove. The rice was half cooked but I was done with it. I turned it away in the trash can and curled up in my room underneath the sheets.

***

I called it the Peace Lily before I even knew the name. At the plant store, I checked the shelves and the plants hidden away behind closed curtains and then when I saw it, I knew. I called it that because of the smell and how, with each sudden breath I took, I felt a certain kind of lucidity. It was a drive away from the anger and the resentment which I still felt for the man

I loved. The woman at the front desk offered me a tight smile before pressing a book about plant care in my arms. I paid and then walked all the way to work. In my office, I placed the plant on the table, next to a picture frame of a bird and then leaned back against my chair to watch it. It had the smell of a rushed sunshine and the ground after a rainfall and I loved the smell. Aryana from the news desk came over to my table. She had a sharp expression but I could still see dark circles underneath her eyes.

"Deadlines, right?" I asked her. We were all accustomed to the streak of deadlines and what they took from us. She laughed and touched her cheeks. "I look pale, don't I? I've been working all night."

It came crashing to me. Autumn man had canceled our date because of work and this lady had worked all night. It could mean I was not as interested or invested in work as all of them or there was something else going on.
She handed me papers and I pressed them together on the table.
She leaned in. "Immigration's getting a little tougher, Fidan. Hundreds of people are trying to leave the country but can't. I've given a detailed report about it but sometimes it is heartbreaking."

"I understand," I said. "I'll edit this and pass it across. Good job, Aryana."

She nodded and walked away. I didn't know why she'd want to indulge in a conversation about anything and much less about immigration but after she'd walked off, I started to think about. For what if I could leave the country and start again, somewhere, without my mother or sister or Autumn man? That would hurt but it would also be worthwhile. Because, stuck here, I was nothing. I had a good enough job and a lover who made me feel safe but suddenly, now, all I wanted was to be rid of all these barriers and move into the world as a new individual with bright ideas and mysteries ready to be unraveled. I wanted to be in another country and in another place and be happy without these audacious thoughts. When Autumn man walked in, I sighed deeply and pushed the thoughts deeper into my mind. I knew it wasn't possible but when he looked at me, I thought he was seeing those thoughts and he did not approve of it. He stepped fully into my office and closed the door. With him in, the office felt cramped and I stood and stared at his body. He smelt of lavender and an expensive after shave and I wanted to bury my hands in his hair.

"I tried calling back yesterday," he said with an air of authority.
"And I didn't want to talk," I replied.
He frowned. "Don't be inconsiderate, Fidan."

I yearned for nothing but silence and the preferential smell of my new plant as he said this. I wanted to scream for him to leave the office but if I did, everyone would know about our love affair. We'd managed to keep it a secret.

Autumn man did not work in the firm. He came sometimes because he was needed.— He had a

large company of his own and houses and money and, sometimes, he had a giving hand. I knew
all of this and yet it did not push me forward.
I said to him in a voice that showed no emo-
tion, "I don't think you should be here, Mr. A."
He chuckled but it did not reach his eyes. "Are
we using formalities with nicknames now?"
It sounded terrible the way he said it but I was un-
moved.

"Can I come to your apartment tonight?"—
he asked. —"I'd like for us to talk...in private."
I couldn't allow him dive into my heart with his subtle
words but it was elevating to think that a man like him
could be interested in a woman like me. We were not
to make the relationship too obvious but, for the first
time, I wanted to let go of those restrictions and hit
him and kiss his lips. The thought simply crossed my
mind in a reckless abandon and I drowned.

"Fidan my lover..." His voice slipped and I could
tell there was something on the line right now.
"Tell me I'm welcomed tonight." —"I can't," I said
with bated breath. "I have work to do." I pointed to the papers on my desk and then touched
the corners of my lips. "I'll be too busy tonight."

He stared at me for what felt like minutes and then, he said, "I'll come over tonight.
Make me rice and put on your red lingerie."
He said it with authority, as if he had somehow
come to own me with his kisses and touches. He
did not let me speak. He walked out and I sat and
I inhaled the Peace Lily in hopes it would be able

to calm me. It did not and I did not wonder why. At home, I told myself there was no need to obey him. That man did not own me. He had no right over me. Yet, by evening, I turned on the stove and poured rice in a pot. When it began to bubble and boil, I turned the water away, added salt and water again and placed it back on the stove. When it was ready, I slipped into the bathroom and used my most expensive soap. It smelt of roses and I was certain he would love it. He came as he had said and brought with him a bouquet of flowers.

"Do not be upset by my nonchalant attitude, my love."
I kissed his hands and put the flowers in a vase. In the small dining room, I served his rice in a plate designed with handmade drawings of flowers. He leaned back against his chair and took a spoonful. I watched him chew, thinking about everything and how much I couldn't stop wanting this man.

Then, he looked up at me. "You are beautiful, Fidan." — "Thank you."
"And you smell nice too," he said.
"Thank you."

The subtle shows of gratitude were dutifully spelled out by my lips and I knew I had no control over them. I simply wanted to please him with the words I could speak and withhold the things that could break us apart.

After dinner, I washed the plates and cleaned the sink. Thereafter, he sat against my window sill and wrapped a smoke. He did not talk to me as he did this but when I watched his hands and the careful way he rolled the paper, I could tell he'd done so before. And then it got me thinking: were they also parts of him that I did not know yet? Later he looked up at me with those dreamy, masculine eyes, and I thought I was seeing my father for the first time again.

"I'd like for you to quit work and come work for me instead." frowned, oblivious of his eyes staring deeply into mine. What the heck was he suggesting? I loved my job. I loved the people who worked with me and the stories they brought to my desk. I wanted to see the world, yes, but I also wanted to do it without feeling this wicked guilt in the pit of my stomach.

I stuttered for words to say.

He raised one hand to hush me and quietly, he lit up the rolled up joint and he puffed the smoke out. It sizzled out quickly. He said, "You do not have to reply me now, Fidan, but take your time. I want to inspire you with change. It is what you truly desire." This man did not know me as I thought he did. What did he know about desires? Did he know that I craved independence with the same urgency as I craved the touches of a man? What then did he know?

He started to touch me. This man with the grey hair and the perfect body started to envelop me with his warmth but then I pulled away.

He looked distraught.

"I won't work for you, A,"— I said vehemently. I could not imagine a world with him around as my boss and I needed him to know that for a certainty. "I won't work for you, ever." He arched an eyebrow and puffed out another smoke. I thought he would choke me with the smoke slithering above his face but he did not. "Don't take your chances, Fidan."

"What the hell do you mean?" I threw back at him. I was done keeping mute. I needed to be heard and I wanted to assure myself that he would. "You will work for me," he said again. There was almost an air of authority in his voice and I was immediately left with a raging question: when did Autumn man own me?

"What do you take me for?" I asked. My voice had risen, I knew. It was to be the first time I'd scream at me. I didn't know it was not and could never be the last. Helookedatmebrieflyandthenglanceddownathisjoint.

"Answer me for goodness sake," I yelled. "I don't know where you live. I've never been close enough for you." "You are childish… and no, I don't mean it as an insult to you or to anyone else for that matter," he responded.

He threw the smoke away and stood and dusted the creases off his shirt.

It was an unexpected retort but after he had said it, I suddenly felt a painful kind of relief; as if it was what I wanted all along. He said, "Surely you can't be contented as an illustrator all your life. Try something else, Fidan, work for me." I had flung a scarf over my hair before he'd appeared but since I'd done so in a hurry, part of my hair was out. I touched it now as he said those words and I felt how stiff they'd somehow become. When he stepped closer to me, I breathe in the scent of his skin and I knew why I craved for him on nights where the loneliness became a daring problem. He smelt terribly good and, for a while, I was entranced by it. I caught myself quickly and stepped away from him. "Let's make our relationship public, A. I want to know you fully. I want to know you."

"But you already know me," he said.
"No, I don't."

We both said nothing. I looked at his face and into his eyes and I wondered if, perhaps, what I'd done was to safely push this man away. Then, the idea of leaving the country and this world that I knew came again to me like a crushing tide and I thought, for a moment, it would bury me alive.

"Let me in, A," I whispered.
I saw him nodding, knew there was more to that than met the eye but said nothing.
He sighed. "I'll do all that you've told me, Fidan," he said.
His voice was low, as though he was exhausted which he most probably was. "Let us make the relationship public in the way that you want."

I nodded. "Sure, let us do that."

I didn't know what to think, this was all uncharted territory for me. Even though technically I knew I was in love with him, I couldn't exactly accept it. He was exotic in the way wild cats were, to be loved from afar but never close enough to touch. Never close enough to shatter the tranquility you've begun to accept as a factor of your existence.

"Fidan… I want you tonight. I crave you." Autumn man said, his eyes two pools of sincerity. I could see him; really see him. He was beautiful in the way he wasn't meant to be, like a wild cat stalking its prey.

"I want you too, I do. But, I don't know." I trailed off as his eyes found mine, boring into my soul. He was pulling me apart without words, his gaze setting fire to my insides.

"Let me be with you. To officially become an item. I want to kiss your tears until they stop falling and alleviate your fears with my fingers caressing your face. You're not meant for mediocrity, Fidan. Can't you see that? Let me teach you… what it's like to truly be alive." His words hit me resoundingly, words I've always wanted to hear.

"I'm yours," I muttered, a whisper he latched onto like the sole survivor of a sinking ship. He was beautiful. Even in the dim light, I could see his perfect body and the grey hairs that added to his allure. Autumn man was beautiful in a way he wasn't meant to be, a being of flawless grace.

"Today, let's put the issues behind us, I want to

know you as one would a woman. It's just us, man, and woman. Place your hand on my chest, Fidan. Do you feel the quaking of my heart? I care about you, more than you know. Lose yourself to me, even if it's just this once." Autumn man was convincing, he always was. He knew what buttons to push to make me go on my knees. Before I knew what was going on, he was standing in front of me, partially unclad.

"Touch me, Fidan. Feel what I feel for you." He guided my hands up to his firm chest, placing them firmly on his chest. His heart was racing, much like he was a teenager on a joyride for the first time. I liked it, I liked it very much. He was open to me, and I knew that I wasn't going to let the opportunity pass me by.

My hands framed his well-sculpted body, as I swallowed surreptitiously, unable to come to terms with the fact that the man in front of me was at my mercy. It seemed ludicrous to think about.

"I want you. Can you feel it?" He said, making me look up at those eyes that seemed to house something too mysterious for me to grasp. But then, I didn't want to. His secrets were his and mine were mine, just the way it was always meant to be.

"Touch me. Touch me the way you wish." I said, allowing him to lead. He wasn't brash, he never was. He slowly unhooked my bra and watched it fall to the floor along with the dress I wore. His eyes followed the movement, sizing me up from top to bottom as though that was the first time, he was seeing me.

"You're beautiful, Fidan. More beautiful than the stars in the sky. Can you feel that? Do you know how beautiful you are? With your body like sculpted glass, a masterpiece. Allow me to worship that which you are, Fidan. Just for today." He said, eyes glazing over with a primal need that made the atmosphere charge almost immediately. I was panting for breath by then, unable to believe that someone like Autumn man could shatter my preconceived notions even without laying a finger on me. His words ran through my body like electricity, sizzling hot. I couldn't keep still. But then, who could have in my position?

"Just for today." I managed to say, my words coming out in a breathless gasp. He placed his hand on my firm breasts, cupping them with his fingers. His hands were gentle, even though his eyes were glazed over with need. He was holding onto me with such carefulness, I felt as though I was porcelain or glass. One that would shatter at any provocation. I liked It, I liked It very much. I was meant to be there, at that moment.

"Fidan.." he trailed off as my fingers landed on a nipple and lightly squeezed. He let out a breath through his mouth, his breath coming in ragged gasps. In that moment, he was at my mercy and there was nothing more beautiful than that. I basked in that moment, not wanting to be eluded by it even for a second. That was my moment, and there was nothing on earth more beautiful than that.

I framed his face with my hands, and he raised me almost with a casual gesture, his eyes boring holes into my body. I was practically unclad before him, but I felt nothing like shame or inhibitions, I wanted to be as wild as lions, I wanted to consume him whole, leaving no crumbs. He didn't know what I intended for him because he looked at me almost in shock, wondering when I became that bold. I didn't want the words to be said, tomorrow was going to take care of itself, however it wanted. But at that moment, I was going to take liberties as much as I dared.

"Shush. Don't say a word now. Just feel." I said to him as he opened his mouth as though to speak and promptly shut it again. I was drunk with the power I wielded over him, and I didn't want it to end. It was my moment, not just his. It was ours.

"You-.." he made as though to speak again but I didn't even blink as my lips found his and I crashed mine onto his in a fiery kiss that left the both of us completely breathless. By then, he was standing in just his briefs, staring at me with something akin to fascination in his eyes. I could tell that he never expected such from me, I was meant to be the calm Fidan, the Fidan who never took charge but was always told what to do. But I didn't want to be that Fidan for that day, I killed her; albeit temporarily.

"I didn't think you had it in you," Autumn man teased, grabbing me from underneath, his hands framing the swell of my bottom, making me elicit a response I didn't want to. He was trying to turn tables and regain control but at that moment, I knew that I wasn't going to relinquish authority to him unless he wrested it from me and even then, I didn't intend to go down easy, not without a fight at the very least. If it came down to it, I was going to hold onto the last shred of me that I had a semblance of control over. As long as that place existed, I wasn't going to be overtaken by the whirlpool that was Autumn man.

I squeezed his nipples again, my fingers framing his face, making those experienced eyes continuously stare at me as though I were a ghost or something akin to it. I didn't mind, it wasn't in my place to. Autumn man was trying to get one up over me as he laid me on the bed and showered kisses all over my face, making me distracted enough for him to gain a semblance of control over himself.

"Fidan, Fidan, Fidan... when did you get so wild? I like, I like it very much. But know whom you do that with, and it's definitely not me." He said, staring right through my soul as his fingers found my wetness and plunged them into me and I cried out, pleasure sizzling up my spine. He didn't seem like he was enjoying himself, he seemed like he was doing it for the sake of superiority.

"You're not meant to go against me, even sexually. Don't you understand, Fidan? I lead, you follow." His fingers plunged straight into my wetness, making my eyes roll into the back of my head. While he did that, a finger of his played with my nipples, making the pleasure compound beyond anything I'd ever felt. It was a tsunami, a storm, an avalanche. It was everything mind-shattering and he wasn't even in me yet.

"I'm yours..." I managed to say, my words coming out in husky breaths, trying without any headway to make sense of the situation I found myself in and somehow get control of the entire thing. Autumn man didn't seem like the type of person who'd let me do that, he wasn't even letting me think. It was a kind of brutality I didn't understand then, it was making a statement with my body.

"Good you know that." He said, staring at me with an unreadable expression on his face. He wasn't a man of many words, from what I saw. But he was a man of expressions, a man who knew what he wanted and went after It. He was an apex predator, one that never understood what it was like to be dominated. She wasn't even sure he could understand even if she tried to explain.

"What would you have me do for you?" He phrased the question like she had a choice even though deep down, she had no single choice. She wasn't a fan of that, but she rolled with it anyways. He was her Autumn man and even though he wasn't always perfect, he was just what she needed. Maybe. She wasn't sure because well… Autumn man had a controlling streak. It was sometimes beautiful and other times…

"Let me see you." I managed to say between gasps of pleasure. He knew just how I liked to be touched and he took his liberties. It was too much for me as his fingers grazed my nipples, much like I did to him earlier.

"Say the words, Fidan. Say you want me more than anything else. More than anyone else. Say it, Fidan." He stared at me, his words pulling me down under.

The intensity of his gaze, and the casual way he said those words that set me afire. Autumn man knew how to use his words, even better than I thought. I was tempted to relinquish all hold on myself and just let him have me, all of me, no takebacks. So, I let go of the reins I held way too tightly, scared to let anyone lead. That day, I was Fidan, the loved. And I allowed myself to bask in it.

"I want you. I crave you. Have me however you wish." I said and I watched his eyes glaze over in need, and there was no longer a need for words or anything like that. No, as at that moment, we spoke with our bodies, letting our hands speak the language our mouths were too scared to.

When his lips covered one of my nipples, I almost lost it. His tongue was warm on me, warm and steadily getting hotter. I was taking leave of my senses, letting his tongue take me to worlds unknown. I'd never been touched that way, not even in my life. It was different from everything I'd ever experienced, anything I'd ever let myself experience.

His movements were unhurried, they always were. It was as though he knew just what I wanted and did his best to make sure there were no complaints. But then, who could complain about such a gorgeous man, no matter how domineering he was? I let him lead, not bothering to guide him. His fingers were still in between my legs and the heat emanating off there could practically cause global warming. I didn't know how I'd never experienced such before because it seemed sacrilegious. How could something so beautiful and wild—untamed in every form, exist without my knowledge? I wanted to know more, to feel more. I couldn't let it pass me by. Not on my life.

He stopped suddenly and before I could ask why or even say a complaint, I felt something huge trying to prod into my wetness. I raised my eyes to stare at him and he looked at me, unsmiling. Then, he plunged himself into me.

Stars exploded in my vision. Even though I'd had sex before, that day seemed extra special, as though he was claiming me, my body, and my soul. He moved like a purebred stallion atop me, moving with such surety, such grace. He was beautiful—magnificent, even. He was a picture of everything a man should be and at that moment, I couldn't even undertake the feelings welling deep within me. Autumn man had somehow scrambled my brain and I couldn't string two words together. My words were coming out in babbles, but I didn't mind, the pleasure didn't need coherent speech. It was all-encompassing and over-whelming. I couldn't even take a breather without feeling like I was being turned inside and out.

I screamed as I felt my orgasm approaching and thankfully, he didn't shy away from it, he embraced it wholly. In fact, he began to move faster atop me; making me moan as hot pleasure ran through me, blinding me for a second. I was lost, completely.

When I came to, Autumn man was gone from the room. I stretched my hand over the bed, but I just met the empty space where he was meant to be. I didn't stand up from there, not for any reason.

There was no point to it, seeing as what was so magical to me was just a passing fancy for him. Not even worth the mention. I couldn't believe I was stupid enough to believe that he was going to stay. Even with the issue that we had earlier, I expected the sex to at least start everything on a clean slate. Autumn man didn't regard me, it was clear. It was all done because he wanted to be. Autumn man was definitely beautiful and everything but... he couldn't stay.

For anyone.

For the first time in a long time, I did not know what to wear. We hadn't come out as lovers before and this new freedom weighed me down. At work, I'd kept a safe distance from Autumn man and he'd respected that in a professional way. Now, though, things were different. Of course I couldn't tell if he had offered for this exposure as a result of the fight we'd had but I did not care. I loved him in the only way I could and as such I had become a willing participant in his affairs. Autumn man had sent the address. I should meet him up at a park. I'd visited the park a thousand times before but when he spelled it in his message, it seemed different and exotic. Perhaps with him I'd feel superbly beautiful and seen and I'd enjoy this experience fully. Autumn man reminded me of the seasons; how easily times changed and people came and people left. He was not cold but he was not hot either. It was irreversible. He was everything in between. I put on long trousers and a shirt and then, finally, I added a long jacket. When I covered my hair with my favorite hijab, I thought about my lover and I immediately felt weak in the knees. In truth, I didn't know what to expect from him wanting to make our relationship public. I didn't know anything anymore. I met Autumn man at the park. He looked manly and unrecognizable standing against the sun. Two teenagers moved past and a man shouted at his little child. Autumn man waved me over and I stepped clumsily through the soft grass, nervous as it grazed my feet.

He did not wrap his arm around me even though it was what I craved for. We were in public. Later, both of us found ourselves walking through the park like two lost children. We did not talk about the weather and about how beautiful the sun was. It was a fine day and a lovely afternoon but none of us was willing to bring that up. We sat down on a bench and he bought sweets. I stuck one underneath my tongue because I wanted to savor the taste of something that wouldn't last. It came to me then that alot of things always found a way of slipping away and I needed to taste and feel before letting go. Suddenly, he placed his hand in mine and raised my hands so he could it. My fingers were painted a dark shade of blue. He trailed his fingers along my skin and chuckled.

"I haven't seen this color on you," he said. His voice was shaky and, no, I could not say why. "Do you like it?" I asked him. He nodded before the words left his lips. "They suit you, Fidan. Everything suits you."

I wondered what was appropriate to tell him and then, when I could not come up with anything, I smiled instead. *Anyone would mistake it as a plea: do not stop trying to appease me. I'm nothing without your sweet talk.*

"Look, Fidan," he said. "I was thinking..."

I held my breath. I was more nervous than I ever was and it confused me. What was it about this man that angered me and yet kept pushing me in? What was it about autumn that broke trees, pressing grasses down like perfumed bracelets?

"What is it, A?" I asked when he stopped.

He looked at me with those piercing eyes and I knew, oh, I knew, that he'd leave and I would again be lonely and empty and depressed. It was as if the end appeared in those eyes like a new beginning and I bathe in it like a sleep deprived teenager.

Wouldn't it be so much better if I left instead of him? Wouldn't it make me happier if I broke his heart before he did mine?

He swallowed. "I'd like to meet your family, Fidan."

I didn't know what to say. Did I tell him I'd promised to go see my mother and I had failed? Did I tell him I was terrible with keeping up with family and those sort of relationships?

"Say something, Fidan," he said. "Now that we are both ready to bring this relationship out, I should meet your family."

It sounded fair but then again, I needed to be in control; needed to be the one in power.

"It's good, A," I said. "But I don't know where you live. I haven't gone to your company once and I don't know about your family."
He sighed and said nothing. Just last night, I had laced the conversation with a need for me to know him deeper. When I looked at him now I could tell it was what he wanted to point out.

"I don't know what you expect from me," I threw past his shoulders.

He looked at me now with a passion unlike what I was used to and he kissed my fingers gently. "Come home with me tonight. Then, tomorrow, I'll take you anywhere you want." I nodded. The sweet had melted under my tongue but I could still taste the bittersweet remainder and it was devastatingly raw.

He drove us in his expensive car down the streets and I pushed one hand out to feel both the sun and the wind and everything in between. Ibrahim Tatlises' song was playing on the radio so we did not need to fill the car with unnecessary talk. I had a lot to say, however, but I did not dare bring it up. I did not want to spoil the mood with questions as to why he wanted to see my family. I thought about my mother and her calloused hands and then I thought about my sister harboring secret thoughts of a world different from one she'd come to know and then I thought about my father.

He was the distant one. He was never around. He was not my father.

"What are you thinking about?" His hand came to touch mine slightly. His eyes remained fixated on the road but I could tell that there was some sort of imbalance in them, as if he was rightly afraid of looking at me.

"About us," I said. It was not the truth. I was thinking about home and the trees at the back of the house which would bend and bloom as the seasons changed. I was thinking about a long streak of broken memories.

But I couldn't tell him all that.
"We are good as we are, Fidan," he said.

I agreed without thinking.

"Don't think so much," he said again and I nodded. After a while, he leaned in and he asked, "Are you happy?"

I immediately began to think about my mother and the question she'd asked me a long time ago in Turkish. What indeed was happiness? Was it a covered up expression of a million guilty thoughts? Was it someone else's careless touch and a plea for surrender? Was it simply the calling of his name? You know how when you listen to a song, you feel the weight of the world all at once and as it envelops you, it takes the oxygen away. How, as the song dips, you feel a type of euphoria that breaks your heart and makes you, in a way, want to live and die at the same time. I've felt that way in the calling of his name. I have been awakened in that mundane expression of intensity and as he asked that, I instinctively whispered his name.

"What?" he asked.

I shook my head.

"Are you happy with me, Fidan?"

I did not know for sure. There were times where his presence both irritated and excited me. There were times when his touches did not leave a feverish ache in my body. Those were the times I did not find happiness anywhere with him. But I couldn't tell him all that; could not start the long streak of explanations and framed smiles.
Instead, I answered in a practiced lie. "I am happy with you; always have been and always will be."
I said it as though there was a future between us even though I knew I would soon go away. I said it as though I meant it.
We passed people selling their wares and Autumn man stopped for me to buy some shawls. We got to my place and we settled down on the kitchen floor. I saw that he closed his eyes and then I studied his expression as best as I could. There was, of course, nothing written there.
He looked somewhat different in the glow of glow of the kitchen's artificial lights and I couldn't but think that, in a year or two, if I stayed with him still, I'd become quite like him. He was good but that striking

mystery was gone, replaced simply by his indiffer-
ence to certain things.

He pulled his eyes open and I saw that they were a
dark shade of blue and not grey as I'd first thought.
It was impractical that I would make such an alarm-
ing mistake about something so infinitely small but I
had done so and now, alone with him, I understood
fully that I did not know him and he did not know
me.

"I have made some mistakes in my lifetime, Fidan,"
he said to me. His gaze had lowered to his hands and
I saw that he was knitting it in a distinct pattern. I
watched it carefully until I grew bored and couldn't
classify it as an innocent art of creativity. He was
nervous and that was it.
"What kinds?" I asked him.

I was thinking about the kinds of mistake I too had
made as a young child and how, on each breathless
occasion, my mother had hit me and then warned
me. Once, I'd broken her favorite vase and then next
time, I'd almost drowned my little sister. I stared at
Autumn man. Were those the kinds of mistakes he
too had made?

He shifted his weight again and sighed. "I was
stubborn and didn't do as I was told. I thought I was
better than everyone else and when it hit me that I
really wasn't, heck, it was late."

"But you are still successful," I said to him. "You are
a successful and intelligent man, still."
"I am not," he said.

And I wondered if he was talking about himself or
me; whether he was deliberately bringing this up
to effectively thwart any plans I would make or was
making to leave as well.
When he went back home, I made warm milk and
drank from it and stared at the stars as they slowly
began to appear.

When it came down to effectively loving a person
with the whole of your heart, I found that Autumn
man was lacking. I could see, from his actions and
words, that he was learning how to love me. I saw
that. Yet there was an infinite amount of longing
when he looked at me. He did not love me as I loved
him and it hurt me more than anything else in the
world.

I decided to leave first. He had the power to drag
me down if he so wanted but I was done feeling
as though I was nothing but a mere discovery that
would soon become worthless. Sometimes I would
feel comfortably fragile with him and other times,
he'd turn me into a portrait of someone he used to
know a long time ago. It was both annoying and sad
and frustrating. I wanted out.
I did the one thing I could: I started to save. I studied
the write up on migration and thereafter decided I
would go to Canada and grow and become happy. It
was a decision I made one day, alone in my apartment.

I would not start small but I would be wise in the
methods of saving. It wasn't that Autumn man was
necessarily terrible but suddenly I was afraid of his
hands on mine. He would not intentionally hurt me

but his presence now became like drowning; as if, now, ten thousand people were pressing me underneath a body of water. I could breathe and then I couldn't. If I thought deeply about it, I knew I was also at fault. For too long I'd bent forward towards his thoughts and wills and I'd relegated mine to the background because I wanted to please him. When Autumn man pleased me, it was because a part of him would be in favor too. He was devoted to me in halves and while that kind of love was satisfying for any other woman, it was not for me.

I'd grown up in a family where love had felt forced and obligatory and seeing something real and different from someone else had awaken within me a sense of happiness. Yet I was far from satisfied. I needed more, craved more than just a kiss or a pat in the back. I needed to be free in the world, bathe in sunshine and multicolored universes and revel in the layered mystery of the world. I needed love that was full and real and honest. I wanted everything I couldn't have. I don't think I was ever content in the things that I had. I was always in search of more and ultimately, I could tell it would become the end of me. I didn't care, however, because the thing with dreams was that it always did find a way of allowing a person play with words and diverse realities. I began to save in bits. I shared it. I would save and then also use the rest to pay the bills and stay alive. Autumn man bought a bouquet of roses and a box of chocolates one evening and as I set the table, ready for dinner, he eased gently to my side and kissed my shoulders.

He whispered my name and it sounded like a prayer.

"I adore you, don't you know?" He asked in a strange voice. It was not his and yet it did not bother me. I turned to face him. His face looked older but he was still so handsome. There was a fine line between his arrogance and humility sometimes and, as I had simply discovered, it bubbled to the surface depending on his mood.

Tonight, however, he seemed excited as if there was news he couldn't wait to say. He took my hand in his. This time around, we were not outside where laws and restrictions could push or weigh us down. We were in my apartment with the high windows and the whitewashed walls and he could hold my hand if he so pleased.

"Are you content with me, Fidan?" he asked.

I frowned. What if he had somehow come to know about my plans to flee? Because, yes, I called it fleeing. If I was running away from work and his tied down love and my family without all of their blessings or knowledge, then it was fleeing. That was what I was planning to do even if I knew it would wildly be one of the hardest decisions I'd take in my lifetime.

"What do you mean, A?" I asked him instead. He let me go and ran a hand through his hair. "Do I make you happy? Do I make you feel like a woman now?"

When have I ever told him I didn't feel like a

woman without him?— I was a woman long before he ever walked in and I would be a woman long after this relationship dissolved. I pushed away from him and swallowed. Still I couldn't bring myself to say those words to him. Not now, anyways.

" Fidan —" he stopped himself. "I want to make you happy and satisfied. I want to give you everything."

I nodded silently like a little child, vexed that he would think so lowly of me in any form.

"Quit your job," he said. It was not a suggestion. "What do you mean quit my job?" I knew what he meant but this time I was ready for an attack. I'd be unable to save up for my travel if I stopped work now but he would not understand. "I have money," he said. "I'll buy you jewelries and walk you through the ends of the earth." I stopped him with the wave of a hand. "You know, for someone as intellectual as you are, I expected more."

He looked too stunned to speak. We stared straight at each other like wounded animals. I could feel both his shock and anger reflected in the corners of his eyes and I could feel my nervousness on the tip of my tongue.

"So I don't make you happy and contented?" He asked after a while.
"I am not talking about being happy and contented," I screamed at him. "I don't want you to flatter me or act like my father. Don't you know it's tiring?"

He eased closer and he grabbed my hand and he pushed me closer to his body. I could feel both the coldness and the rawness of his frame and how his hold resembled that of my mother and I did not like it. I shuffled my feet and tried to wriggle my arms away from his hold but his touch was firm and he was angry at the words which I had just spoken.

"Let me go," I said to him.

This man could overpower me without much effort and for the second time this night, I became well aware that I was a woman and I was not growing standing in a position where he could weigh down on me if he so much as moved an arm.

He did let me go but my arm had become sore. He looked at me and then started to apologize over and over again as if he was only just realizing he'd come so close to breaking us. I could see that he loved me; could see that in the in between of our relationship, he wanted the best for me. It was a shame I had more in mind than the love he was ready to dish to me in small doses.

"Please, Fidan," he whispered.

His hands were pressed firmly together like in a prayer and I hated and loved him all at the same time and with the same reckless balance.

"You should leave," I said to him. "I want to be alone, A."

He was nodding before his lips pressed the words

out. "Of course, Fidan. I'm sorry, my love." Then he was gone. It was our first big fight and would be the first of many delicately put in place to break us. At this time, I had no idea and neither did Autumn man.

***

Autumn man sent a card with a handwritten apology. I read the words twice in my apartment and then stared defiantly at the way he had crossed the T's in his note. It was in both English and Turkish. I read the Turkish words first, afraid he'd overdone it but it was good enough. He called me back two hours later.

"Are you still upset with me, Fidan?" he asked.

I shrugged, knowing that he wouldn't be able to see me.

"Are you still there, Fidan, my darling?"
"Yes, I am," I said. "I am not upset anymore, A."
"Can I come over then?" he asked.
I told him no without hesitation.

He said, "Well…do you want to come to my place? I'll send you the address. I know I have promised to take you. Please…"

I wanted to tell him no but then I hesitated and he found an answer. "I'll send you the address now." Three minutes later, my phone beeped and I got the address. I put on my best dress and covered my hair in a hijab before locking all the doors to my apartment. I thought I won't be needing to wear hijab anymore. Soon I will be leaving the country.

It took me over an hour to get to his place but at the door, Autumn man welcomed me with a smile that stole my breath away.

"Come in," he urged in his playful voice.

When I stepped in, I noticed how different the place was and I laughed at the picture of my face framed on the wall. He took my jacket and hung it and then he kissed my shoulders. I began to understand that it had become a ritual for him to kiss my shoulders and I couldn't fault him because it had now become my ritual to hate and love him with the same effortless swell. He kissed my cheeks next with a tenderness that surprised me. He'd already set the table and so we sat down to eat.

It tasted delicious and it was what I pointed out to him after I ate the first spoonful.

"Thank you, my love," he said.

It therefore reminded me of my mother and my promise to go back home to her. Would it matter that days and weeks had gone by and I probably would never go back?

"I think there must be a subtle yet major change between us, Fidan, don't you think so too?" I paused, dropping my knife noisily in the process. "What?"

He smiled. "We've been going out for weeks and months. Don't you think it's high time we call this what it is?" He was searching my eyes for an answer.

It was difficult to get one because I was blank. I was surprised by his question. I knew we shared something special and just like I never expected the first conversation, I didn't see this coming.

I cleared my throat and found my voice.

We had our eyes on pure gold, on moments that should have been cherished in private. On moments that I would remember much later and which would invariably make me question what my motives were, it would feel sickening real. What was I trying to achieve then? One thing was sure. I was genuinely happy, and I wondered why I was trying to end it before it bloomed fully. I wondered why I was trying to crush a budding dream. It didn't have to happen all at once. It was one step at a time. And that was one thing about happiness, it comes when you least expect it. It meets you unprepared and unready to try again. It shuts all doors with negative thoughts and makes you believe you're at the center of it all. But it doesn't always last long. It's temporary. It's short-lived. One moment, you alone matter, and the next, the universe deserved nothing but pure pain and misery because it has given you your share in heaped cups.

"What do you say?" He asked again. "I see a future with you, Fidan. You're a smart and intelligent woman. You have it all together, and even though it doesn't look like it at the moment, I can assure you that it's all going to work out fine. You're going to excel in everything you do. I'll hold your hands through it all, for as long as you let me. I want to see it all happen."

There are people of value and importance that you can call and wake up at four in the morning. And right now, he was just that to me. Not going with him through the twists he now offered in a platter of gold would be a threat to me; A threat to the life without accident that was in front of me.

"I don't know what to say, A."

I glanced around. Soft music was playing from the living room. Everything was perfect. He had planned everything. He had made sure everything was perfect.

The dining room, decorated to my taste. The scents of the candles were just the way I loved them. How could I say no to this?

"Do you like it?"

I started to tear up. No one had ever done something like this for me before. Not even Umer from college. Autumn man had not fully declared his love for me yet and he was going the extra mile to ensure I said yes to him. He wanted to be with me and I didn't see a reason why it should not happen.

"I don't know what you're offering," I laughed. "But yes to whatever it is."

Yes, to the disaster ahead of us. Cheers to heartbreak and lost identities. Yes, to the Autumn Man I won't be able to recognize in years to come. Fingers crossed... Cheers.

***

I called him A. It was short for Autumn, of course, he was my Autumn Man. The dictionary says that apart from being a season, the time or period when someone or something is past its prime is autumn. Years of experience reflected in everything he did. From managing our lives to resources, to how he talked about life like he had experienced it from different dimensions. I believed everything he said. I took his word for it. It didn't seem only like the right thing to do, but the only way to go about things. But he could have any woman he wanted. He didn't need to go after a lowly illustrator.

"Have you thought of quitting your job yet?" he asked one afternoon. I shook my head. It was not true. I had thought of quitting my job a thousand and one times, but it didn't seem like the right thing to do. He asked that I come live with him and rule his empire. How far was that going to get me?

"I want to work for myself, A. I want to grow. I appreciate all you do for me and I know I'm the luckiest woman in the world. I want to build for me. I want to earn everything I have. I'll work for it all. I won't work for you, A. I'd rather not."

"It'll be much easier that way," he tried again.

"Which is the more reason for me not to? I'll continue there, A. I promise you I'll be the best I can."

In a bid to make me a better person, he pushed me too hard sometimes. Too afraid I'll break beyond repairs on some occasions, I would return to my shell. As much as he motivated me, I was afraid of him in times like that. I was his best investment, he'd remind me. One that wasn't going to last long. There was no liquidity, and no use cases to this asset called Fidan. What was the investment about?

***

I felt the warmth and heaviness of something on my chest. The warm feeling disappeared as soon as it came and was replaced with a bit of coolness. I touched it with my hand. He wore an emerald necklace around my neck. My heart was pounding. This man had cast a spell. I turned to him. I was in his arms, without being able to open my lips.

He said in my ear: I love you. And I did not know what to tell him to satisfy the softness and longing in his eyes. He pushed me more.

It was the first time he would be telling me he loved me and it both excited me and pushed me down to limits that neared dying. What did he hope to gain? That I'd stay? He had two sides to him and days and weeks with him had shown me all of those. There were days when his love bloomed like sunflowers. In those days, we'd lie awake on my bed or on his and we'd link fingers together. He'd tell me about his sisters; how he loved them but they were close to distant in his life. He would tell me about the times when they would upset him and he would stand in the sun for hours in fear that he would lose his balance. He would tell me about his mother and her delicious pancakes; how she'd somehow learned to inject snippets of foreign lifestyle into her household.

"Did you learn everything from your family?" I asked one night. He shifted and turned to stare at me. "They taught me how to love, really, but I taught myself who to give it to and how to know they were worthy of it." I swallowed. Did he think I was worthy of his love? I was going to give up on him and his halved love and he did not know that so perhaps, in a way, that night I therefore regarded him as someone who did not know anything.

Still, I voiced out my thoughts. "Do you think I am worthy?"

He nodded without hesitation. "Of course I think you are," he whispered. "You are more than worthy."

I wanted to meet his family but I knew that by suggesting we met his, I'd be inclined to take him to mine and I did not want that. I could already picture my mother with her accusatory eyes. She would drag me up to her room and shut the doors and hit my shoulders repeatedly.

"But he's so much older than you," she would say. "I know, ma," I would tell her to her face.

And then, I wouldn't come back home again and she wouldn't call or miss me. It was to be the ways of the world as well as my family dutifully confined to things they had known for far too long. I wanted, no, needed change and I would get it either way.

"I love you, Fidan," he said.
"Love you too," I replied.

I was deftly afraid of fading out before I ever got the chance to shine brightly so I avoided telling him I loved him. Instead, I broke the love message by removing the I in the statement. He did not understand. A question would always come at me and would immediately thrust into my skin: How can you wake up one day and see someone suddenly enter your life? First you want to keep your distance; you do all that is within your power to restrain your heart. But without realizing it, you become so captivated by its magic that all your definitions disappear from the borders and in the whirlwind that it has created for you. You have no choice but to cling to yourself so that the storm of your emotions does not overwhelm you.

How did I get here?

I wrote this in my journal, underlining the question with four unsteady markings. I had bought the brown journal weeks before A had proclaimed his love for me and with it, I had written my feelings and thoughts and fears. With the journal in place, I could almost always lay down my fears and shed my skin. I could hide from the world and still be as powerful as I never was. I wrote down I was scared of Autumn man. I wrote that I loved him with passion I had never come to understand. I wrote down I did not trust him. And when I would curl up to sleep, I would think about those words and those writings and I would tell them to myself in a comical way so that it would not sting too much. I lost the journal on the day I wanted to cancel out that I did not trust him. It wasn't there on the table or beneath my pillow. It wasn't under the bed or beneath the sheets. I had lost a part of myself and I could not tell what hurt the most. When I met with A and I told him about the missing journal, he held my hand.

"What do you need it for anyway?" he asked. "You could always talk to me."

I hit his hands and he dropped them. It would be the first time I was attacking him. I was normally the meek and gentle woman who could shove love into his throat with a golden spoon but now, I was no longer recognizable. I was a woman who'd had the audacity to strike him and he did not look pleased. I was the one who apologized. I was the one who boiled rice for him and kissed his neck.

***

"Am I qualified to meet your family now?"

I had grown tired of hearing this question. It was draining and uncomfortable. I didn't want to talk about my family. I didn't want to have anything to with floating roots. They didn't go as deep as they were supposed to. They hung in the air, suspended by strife and rejections.

"This is not about you, A." I sighed for the tenth time that evening. "If it were up to me, I'd have introduced you to my family after our first conversation,"

"But you didn't," he cut in. He sounded annoyed.

"And I have my reasons, A."

"How far do you think we can go with this if connections like this are not made?"

"There's nothing I can do about it now, A. I'm no magician. I don't know how to cast spells. I don't know how to make people love me all of a sudden. If they didn't do it since, I don't think I can bear the show they will try to put up. I'm not you, A."

I wanted to take the seat beside me when I noticed the journal I had been looking for lying on it. It was a journal I used and had been using for months to detail my particular existence and it had gone missing. I had told him about how I had cautiously searched for it and now I was seeing it in the chair beside him. How had it gotten here?

My heart broke into many pieces. I could feel the color drain from my face. Why was he doing this? Why did he do this?

"I asked if you had seen that journal, A? How did it get there?"

"What journal?" He asked. He followed my line of sight and saw the book covered in red leather sitting on the chair. I didn't want to look accusing. I didn't want to sound so too.

"I don't know what you think I did, Fidan." He said disappointingly.

I wanted to believe him. I really wanted to. I trusted him. I just had to without a choice. He had not given me any reason not to. He was kind, patient, and loving. He only wanted the best for me. But that journal hurt me to the core. It was my life. It knew the sides of me A had no idea of. It was the delicate storm of my body; the me I didn't want anyone to see. It held my vulnerability, much more than he did.

"I don't know what you're talking about, A." I felt my trust beginning to waver. "I have been searching for this book for some days now. I asked if you had seen it and you said you hadn't. How did it get here?" He looked around, searching for what to say. That's not how I had sensed it then. Years ago, it looked like he could not believe me. It looked like he was looking for the best way to contain his anger, and not break into his lies. "I have no idea, Fidan. You might have dropped it there when you came here a few days ago."

I nodded. I was mad, angry and broken. Still I wanted to rest in his arms because he was where I found solace. Little did I know that he was also where my distress was built.

***

How long do you have to wait to know if you've had enough? For how long would you shake your head in silence?

I almost had no mind of my own and he knew that. I'd do what he said was best for me, but for how long?

It took me long enough to decide I wasn't going to put up with him anymore. I may not have known much, but I knew enough to be convinced that this was not the life I was meant to live. I was made for more. I was built for more. This conviction didn't all come at once, but when it did, I embraced it with open arms.

"Have you heard about the conference in Abidjan?"
"Isn't that in Africa?" I laughed. "What would I possibly gain there?"
I found it amusing that he thought I knew so little that Africa would be the best training ground for me.

I think he missed the joke. "You see, this is one of the few problems I have with you, Fidan." "I don't get what you mean. If it's about my question, A, I meant it as a joke." It was his turn to be amused. "No, Fidan. It wasn't a joke." That was where he'd caught me! "I know you well enough to know when you mean something…and I know you meant it."

I didn't understand why that was a problem. It was a joke and we could move past it. Couldn't we?
"Okay?"
"You see; the world is too wide for someone who is as narrow-minded as you are. Yes, you heard that right. There are diverse cultures you need to learn about and many opportunities you need to take up as soon as they come."
"I read a lot on cultures, and you know that. I don't need to visit to know a lot. If the opportunity came, I'd take it up, of course. But for something that wouldn't make meaning to my life? I don't think this

is the time."
"And that is another mistake you're making there.
You see, your job puts you in a tight space. It puts
your mind in a closed box. You can't think of anything outside it. You can't do much outside literature
or feature stories, can you?"

His words stung. I felt like a million daggers were
thrown at me at the same time. Why did he have to
be like this sometimes?
"You could work for me, Fidan. There are a lot of
opportunities waiting for you."
"I'm learning a language already."
"And that's more reason for you to visit Abidjan. It's
an African country that was colonized by…"

And on he went, trying to make me feel like I
know nothing of value. "I know that already."
"Then act like you do. Speak up. Let's have enlight-
ening conversations. Teach me. I want to learn from
you."
"This is totally out of context, A. Where is this coming from?"
He rubbed his temple with the back of his palm. "I
want what's best for you. I want to see you succeed,
Fidan. I want to be by your side when it happens."
"And what if it happens when you're not?" I asked. I
wanted to know what would be his response.
"I'd be happy any way."
"Oh."
"Yes, Fidan. I love you and it's my greatest heart's
desire that you bloom into that beautiful flower that
all would want to see. The world will want to stand

with you. I'll never leave you."

"And what if I don't become all you hope I become? What if your plans are not my plans? What if I want to live life passively and not pay attention to the spotlights?"

He sighed. "I know you do. I made this mistake, and I wouldn't want you to make the same."

And now you want to live your unfulfilled life through me. It was the first time that it dawned on me. A was living his dreams through me. I wasn't narrow-minded. I had all I needed. I didn't want all he wanted for me. It was his problem, and he'll have to deal with it.

I need to run. I need space. I need to be free. I can't be restricted by a man who thinks I should be subject to his every desire. Be free like the bird, Fidan. Flee.

***

I wanted to discover the world. My body ached to see new places. Meet new people. I needed to experience life outside hijab, outside him, and outside Turkey. If I close my heart, I am afraid of breaking myheart. From the horrible feeling of loneliness after his absence. The image of him came before my eyes and his name was on my lips, my heart burned with nostalgia. I guess sometimes in life you cross boundaries and set foot on a path that has no end, but if you do not go, if you do not have a heart, there is no life left for you.

I have to remind myself that what he had to give was not love. Love wrecks you. It makes you that selfless person you never were. A creature that used to be another is now as important as we are. You think for two, make decisions with two minds. However, we have no control over love and him. We are both eager and afraid of love and intimacy. There is an ancient legend about a giant who takes out his heart, puts it in a string of locked metal boxes, and buries them all. In this way, his enemies can attack him with a dagger or a shot, but he will never be killed. Of course, he also loses the benefits of having a heart, that is, happiness. The giant becomes sad, and although he tries to enjoy playing, after a while he feels so miserable that he pulls out his own heart and pierces it with a dagger. Each time I remember this legend, I take joy in knowing I didn't hold back. I learned my lessons; at least for a few years, I didn't give myself to brokenness wearing love as a mask. I had made up my mind. I had to leave, and I didn't care about the cost. I needed to experience peace, and I knew I couldn't have that in Turkey. My escape plan wasn't carefully plotted, but I knew I'd get it right eventually. I knew I'd make it out of this alive. All I had to do was tell him. I needed to break things off with him. I needed to stand my ground and not let him make me feel like I was making the worst decision.

What happened when I left? He'd move on to the next conquest. He'd fall in love again like I never meant anything to him. He had a part of me with him, I knew that. They all did.

***

He was seated in his car waiting for me. I wasn't bold enough to tell him to his face but it had to be done somehow. He had to know. I pasted the text I had type and revised a hundred times before I slept on the text box. I said a brief prayer before I hit the send button. My heart raced, the headache I had earlier was building into a migraine. It could not have been a regular headache from the onset.

" Fidan!"

I heard him call from the door. As expected, he didn't go. He didn't leave. He never listened. "Fidan!"He applied more force on the door this time.

I opened the door. I felt like a traitor who had lost all his possessions and was now a bankrupt character. He gave me all but took more, so I wasn't to blame for it all.
"You may not believe it but I love you and I have to do this for me, A. I have just these ten or twelve days left depending on when I'm called and I'm sorry I didn't say anything earlier. I gave hints and thought you understood. It hurts to think that I could not meet your expectations, A. I'm not enough and I never will be for you."

"I promised you a great life out of Turkey or in Turkey. We could still have that. Go say your prayers. Say the Al-fathia, Fidan. I promise, you'll feel much better after of it. I hoped for the best. I gave you all I believed will take you through this journey of self-discovery. If I was given this kind of head start at life, I'd be a much greater person. I'd have achieved a lot more that I have now."

"No, A. You tried to live your life through me. You gave, but took too much. I couldn't help but think I was living for another. How much longer was I going to continue living that way? You didn't achieve all you would have loved to and you thought the best way to do it was through me. That's why you pushed me."

"You know very well what I'm saying. —I am definitely not satisfied with the previous conditions of my life. I am not. They took thousands of forms of forced labor from me and had unrealistic expectations of me. But is it the way to reach a secret life? I am a stranger to this kind of behavior."

"I'm more a stranger to anything than you are, A. I didn't have and I still do not have that head start you think I do. I only ask that you let me go, A. Forget about me." I wished he would leave at this instant. I was getting intoxicated by his scent and it did me no good. My body ached to be wrapped in his. I wanted to hear about his big plans even for the last time. He looked like he was about to sink. There were tears in his eyes. " Fidan, you are free and you can go without having an obligation to a special person or persons, but you, captured by your own limitations!"

I wanted to yell at him and tell him that wasn't true, but he was right. I hated that this man knew me inside out. He sniffed. "And what is most interesting that I know right now is that you are want something I don't know. Being with you was bliss and enjoyable

but now it is going to haunt me for the rest of my life."
I sobbed quietly and wondered if perhaps I was making a terrible choice. "Why do you want to make me
miserable, Fidan?" he asked. His voice was loud and
shaky and I could tell I'd been the monster to break him.

"But…"

"I know you say you do not know how to draw
love and affection. That's what makes you more
worthy of love. You don't yearn for it. You
don't want it. You don't go chasing after it."

I felt a tear roll down my cheek. "I know I do
not know anything! Even living. It is not a matter of giving up on anyone's hope! I want to be a
little lonely to see if I can continue or not. I have
a headache, A. I need to rest. You should leave."

"You should maybe clear your mind, honey. This
is the only right way for you and me. We can build
from here. Rest and get rid of your little headache. Have you had something to eat today?"

I didn't respond.— I had nothing to say to him. —If
he was not going to leave. —Then we might as well
dwell in silence. "Get something to eat. I'm sure you'd
feel a lot better afterwards. Trust me, it always works."

"I'm done trusting you, A. I'm done believing that
you want the best for me. You might want that,
but you don't know how to show it." I said bitterly.
"You think you know it all, but I'll let you know A,

you don't have it all together. You're as confused as I am." I lied. I wanted to make him feel bitter.

"I do not know Fidan. I cannot curse. I cannot have everything together. So let me follow the one I caused. The one whose fault is with me. I can't let you go, Fidan. I don't think I ever will." He sounded broken, and it broke my heart even more. "It is the most painful decision of my life."

"And we can stop the pain. We can prevent the pain by not going through with this. The power is in your hands."

I shook my head fervently. "No." I could feel his heart sink. I saw that look in his eyes. I could recognize it from myself.
"I'm going crazy Fidan. Do not hurt me more than this."
"We were nothing, A. It's time you believe it and move on. There was nothing special between us. I was nothing to you." The words hung on the ridge of my teeth. It was hard to say them. The damage had already begun. I might just finish it. "We were just another disaster waiting to happen. I should have listened to my mother."
"What does it mean that you were nothing? How comfortable are you with saying that? How could you even think that, Fidan?"

I just wanted to leave. I just waned my peace.

"I'd say you left too easily. You gave up on us too fast." He said after a few moments of quiet had gone by. It was like a minute of silence for our dead relationship.

"I cursed myself a thousand times and got stuck in a loop of endless madness. It was just me and myself, alone in there. I was first losing my mind, and then myself. Then you say I left you so easily?" I broke down in tears.

"What do you think of me, Fidan?" I had no strength to speak, nor the will to do so."You are the craziest and most lovable woman which I have seen in my life," he continued.

I still could not bring myself to say anything.

"You regret this, Fidan " he said with his back to me.

***

I remember waking up early morning from one of the worst nightmares I'd ever had.

It's your mind playing games with you, Fidan. It's all in your head. He's not chasing after you. He won't stop you from chasing your dreams. He can't hinder your freedon. He won't drain you in Canada. You're doing this for you. You deserve peace, and you can have it in Toronto.

When I could just get mentally prepared for the trip? I needed to talk to someone, and Paula was the only available option. I trusted no one else, not even the one I thought I was going to spend my entire life with.

"Hello," she picked on the second ring.
"Did I wake you up?" I felt sorry about disturbing her sleep.

She sighed. "No, you didn't. I've been up all night. You know things have not been easy since my break with Dan." I understood exactly how she felt because I was in the same shoes. It is me up to think I had ruined what might be my only shot at love. "How about you? Have you found someone to take the apartment?" "I saw a few offers on the site but none of them were close to my initial price." I didn't want to talk about me or any of my problems. I'd found a friend in Paula and I hoped she could somehow be sensitive enough to understand that. "How are things with the office?" She paused for a while before answering. "Remember that short man with a wide moustache?" She asked. "Yeah," I nodded as if she could see me. "The one who used to follow me all through my first year. Never knew his name." Paula laughed. "I don't know either." I laughed along with her. Isn't it crazy that we had worked together for a long time and we never spoke until my last days in the office? That was another one of my regrets. With Paul present, there would have been no him. "Well, he got arrested for child molestation yesterday."— "What?" I knew Paula would fill in as the best distraction. "Yes," she giggled lightly. "I'm sorry the children had to go through that, but was he that bad that all the grown up ladies won't go out with him?"

The echoes of her laughter rang through my almost empty room. "You caused this, Fidan. You could have gone out with him for at least one lunch date. It wouldn't hurt." "So he could molest me?   —See how you're now the bad guy, Paula. You don't know what that guy is capable of doing!" "Not worse than A has." She tried to joke. — "It would have been all belly hugs and a couple of cigarettes." "You're lucky you covered that one up really quick. I wouldn't have taken that lightly." — "I know, I know. I'm sorry." Even though I didn't want to talk about my problems I felt she needed to know some things. "I have no exact plans for Canada." I blurted out. "You have got to be kidding, Fidan. What do you plan to do when you get there?" She asked, her voice laced with concern. I threw the phone on speaker dropped it beside me. I lay down and spread my arms across the bed. The same one he held me in a few months ago.

"I have money. I've been saving for quite sometimes and I believe it's going to help me settle in. I'll buy a, rent an apartment, whatever." I sighed. I hadn't really thought this through. But I knew deep down I wouldn't be stranded.

"You'll figure it out, it's going to be a really long trip, you know. You should get some rest." Paula said and yawned. We had been talking for the past three hours and even though I knew she had to be at work in three hours, I didn't want it to end. It was the last time we spoke. She didn't know that, but I did.

I didn't want the memories from Turkey following me to Toronto. I was going there to build a new life for myself. I was laying foundations for my children, if I grew to have any. The chances were slim at that period because I'd grown far away from love, and it from me. I got to the airport, willing, ready, and full of life. I was motivated. This world had nothing on me. I checked in at the first gate, only to read the notice on the screens. Our Turkish Lira which was exchange for the dollar at the rate of 1 dollar to 15.96 Lira had gone up to 49.20 Lira. It was temporary, they said. So why did it have to happen now? How did I not hear about this? "It is not too late to turn back, Fidan. Cancel the flight and request for a refund. You have years to decide on what to do with your life. You have much longer to explore." I shook my head and did a few calculations. I had a lot of money, some of which came from A's extravagant gifts. If I went on with this, I'd be left with $2000 dollars with nothing to fall back on. The money in my escrow account meant nothing. Once again, take a leap of faith, Fidan. You have got this. Deciding to move to Canada was the hardest part of my journey without him. It was the beginning of a new chapter.

As I sat in the plane, I said to myself:
Be courageous

Don't hold back
You deserve everything good, including love
Follow your heart

Let love lead
You are not totally broken, Fidan
Pick up the pieces
Fix yourself up
Remember the sky is your starting point

You don't have to be afraid
You've got this

Believe in yourself

You've seen the real you; Unmask
You have moved past your mistakes
Your past is not bigger than you are

You have flipped through the new chapter:
Be courageous

CHAPTER TWO
The Scent of Incense

My life was set; I was on my way to Toronto. Love was the least of my problems, I didn't care, and my career was my solace. I had a long list of things I wanted to do before I died, love was the least.

When I landed in Toronto, my purse was close to empty. I didn't have much, but I was determined. I wasn't going back to Istanbul; it was too late now. I called a taxi, and told him to take me to the nearest motel. When I got there, I had less than $2000 on me. I thought I was crazy; how could my dreams drive me so much that I'd lose the fact that I hadn't had enough money? He dropped me off this strange motel, it seemed deserted, and there was no single person in sight. If there was a time I felt discouraged, that was the moment. I walked in to the reception, it was stuffy, the motel had electricity, but the only evidence was the light bulb that shone over the counter. I hadn't even reached the counter and I was sweating inside. I remember the receptionist, Maria, a woman that looked in her forties. She was kind, explaining to me that the motel didn't have much luxury that I needed. She offered to give me directions to the next motel down the street smile on her face, it reminded me of my grandma. I declined her offer, and decided I was going to stay with her, so far as it was cheaper, she looked like she needed company. She gave me the key to her best room. It was a little bit cramped, but it was comfortable. I quickly changed and joined her downstairs. "Aren't you supposed to be resting my dear?" she asked, when I dragged the stool to sit with her at the counter. I smiled. "I was bored, I needed company" I said, she winced at me a bit. "You're not from here right?" she asked, passing me a bottle of orange juice. I smiled, she probably must've heard my Turkish accent, even though I was speaking English. I told her why I came to Canada, my hopes to finally start living, and my need for a job. She gave me a list of websites to check, and a café just down the street with free Wi-Fi. I was glad I stopped by Maria's motel.

The next morning, I stepped into the café Maria spoke to me about yesterday with a few bucks in my hand; I ordered a latte and sat at a far end corner. I went through the sites and applied for several positions in different publishing houses that I saw vacancies. I went back to the motel and rested. It was my routine for the next few days. Coffee, check my mail and have conversations with Maria. The highlight of my day was getting to talk to Maria over breakfast. She understood I was running low on money and she always bought food for two. I felt bad about it, but I couldn't help but accept her kind gestures.

Maria couldn't keep the building going and she had some suitable buyers. I saw it coming; I was one of few people in the motel for over three weeks. She did the cleaning, made sure I was comfortable, and even did the repairs herself. She was the handywoman, the plumber and the electrician. Her late husband did actually teach her a lot, but it was a matter of time before the bills became too much to handle. She had no one else. No child, no friend, no one.

I got a job a few weeks later. A publishing house. The pay was not what I wanted, but it was way better than what I earned in Istanbul. My first day at the office, I was so shy. Her smile was so warming and inviting. I summon up courage to walk up to her and extend my hands for a handshake. "Hi. I'm Fidan" I said, with my voice shaking. She got up and hugged me, which took me as a surprise. "Nice to meet you, Fidan, I'm Lara" she says, smiling. She smiled a lot, I thought it was a facade. Months later, I realized that it was her nature. We've been friends, and sisters. We did everything together, lunch, coffee, work and all. She was there. But I lost her for a man.

***

Maria sold the motel, and pleaded I was to be given a few more weeks. They declined. I didn't have much money, and the nearest motel was pricy. I came to work that day, not knowing where to go, with my stuff in the corner. Work was slow that day, but my mind was somewhere else, I needed a place to sleep. Lara saw my mood, and was worried. She moved at me during the break

"What is going on? I've never seen you this sad" she said, dragging me to get coffee. I was silent for a while. Coming out, I saw my stuff being carted away by some displaced people.

"Leave my stuff!" I screamed. Lara was shocked, and didn't understand what was going on. I felt embarrassed, Lara said nothing. She looked at me with grave eyes, like she understood. The rest of the day was silent.

"You know, you could stay with me, my sister just moved out" she said at the end of the day's work. I was shocked. She helped me pack my bags and we got to her apartment, a block down the street. It was a comfy place with two rooms. It still had some packed boxes, but it was perfect. I was grateful for a friend turned sister.

For the next few months we stayed together, worked together, cried together and built together. She was more than a friend. There were a lot of advances from cool people but that was not what I was looking for. There was Rob, the IT guy, Khaled, the marketing guy, even Allen, the mail man. I learnt to smile, yet ignore their advances. I grew in the corporate ladder, and visited Marie every weekend. I finally felt like my life was coming back altogether.

That was when I met him. I remember that day vividly, Lara and I sat together, with a bucket of popcorn, doing a Netflix series when he called. He's been calling frequently during the last year, but I didn't know who he was, and I didn't ask questions. This day was different. I do not know what touched him to video call Lara. She paused the movie and went to the bedroom. I didn't see her for a while, I grew impatient.

"Lara come on! "I said in a pleading tone, dragging her to the living room. She laughed, and said to the man she was on the video chat with.

"Here's my Turkish friend I told you about," she says, pointing the phone directly at me. I'm a shy person, my face flushed as she passed me the phone.

"Hi", I remembered saying. I looked at him and I was bewildered. He was more beautiful than I expected. He had a light skin, dark brown eyes, curly black hair. He caught me unawares, I couldn't hide the shock.

We spoke for a few minutes and I gave Lara back her phone. I went back to the living room and continued the movie without her. I was in some ten minutes later when she came outside, smiling as usual. "He asked for your number," she said casually. I smiled, pretending to not be interested.

"I gave him your number," she said. I acted furious. I ranted for a while about why she'd give my number to a complete stranger I talked to for less than five minutes. She laughed,

"I know you like him too; I see the way you smile" she said teasingly. I laughed heartily. It wasn't long after the movie that I saw his text on WhatsApp.

Adam: Hello Fidan, I'm Adam, nice to meet you

Fidan: Hi, nice to meet you too.

It was supposed to be a "hi" and "hello" conversation, but I remembered we found ourselves texting back and forth till early hours of the next morning. For the next few weeks, I woke up to a lot of good morning texts, and every single one of those warmed my heart. Soon it was not just texts, but flowers, everywhere both at the office, and at home. Soon he was paying for a month's supply of Lunch from the cafe for Lara and me. I felt he was moving way too fast, but I knew I loved the attention. I had to constantly remind myself not to think about him, but I was either texting him, or thinking about him. I wanted to think about the worst things. What if I was being cat fished? What if he had a wife and two kids? Or even stranger, what if he just wanted a friend? I talked to Lara about it. She laughed; shocked that he had not popped the question yet. She then advised me to clear everything, by asking him. I was scared; I knew I wouldn't do it. I contemplated for days. One night, I was fed up and I decided to come out clean, rather than die with those thoughts, I texted:

Hey, I really want to know what's going on. We've been going back and forth for months, what are we doing?

I contemplated sending that message. I was so in love with him that I'd rather be friends than less. I summoned up courage and clicked send.

Typing…

I was scared, did I just ruin things with the only other friend I had? I was sure I wanted to be with him, of course, if he wanted to be with me.

I love you Fidan, I just didn't want to take things too fast with you. I was scared it was too early, and you'd say no.

I smiled. "Love" was a strong choice of word to use. I was in love with him, but how could I be in love with someone I've not met? But, it was genuine, the flowers, the coffee at work, the sandwich for lunch. I hadn't even gone out with him yet and he showered me with all these gifts, he never stopped. He made me want myself, gave me a chance at love, he made me love him. It was mostly exciting and I enjoyed it. I got to know him better, he even began taking this online course on Turkish. He was a successful accountant, in Qatar. I let myself want him, I let myself try. I let my guard down and couldn't stop thinking about him. It was just one week before he set a date. He sent me a flight ticket to come meet him in Dubai. I was shocked. I haven't been outside Turkey all my life. I had been saving some money to get to Canada, but a first class ticket to Dubai?

"You should go," my boss said after he removed his glasses and rubbed his temple. I was nervous, I was just an illustrator, I doubted he'd let me skip work for a few days on a short notice. "Just know what you're doing Fidan" he says. I walk towards him and give him a hug. He smiled. I went through work that day with a lot of enthusiasm. It hit me as I packed, "where was I going to stay?"

I was troubled for a second. It was the first time I was going on a date with him, I didn't want anything silly to happen, so I quickly texted him.

I hope you won't expect me to sleep in your bed, I don't know you that well... I threw my phone on the bed. I really liked this guy; I just hoped I hadn't messed things up. He replied almost immediately.

Don't worry Ms. illustrator, I booked separate rooms for each of us.

I was shocked. Who was this guy that was willing to spend so much on me and respected my boundaries? Why was I falling for him? I can't forget. I remember coming out from the plane down the terminal to see him come pick me himself. He had a valet, but he took my luggage himself. How could a man have so much and be so humble? His hands were in mine as we drove to the hotel. He then gave me my keycard and set the date for eight pm. I lay on my bed thinking how the day played out, wondering if this was real, or if he was just a dream. I knew it was reality when I pinched myself a couple of times and felt pain.

I was in the hotel's restaurant at 7:58 PM, and he was already seated. I never had met a man so organized and time conscious. There was lots of wine and Asian foods. I couldn't remember what happened after I dragged him to the dance floor, I just knew I woke up in his room, covered with the duvet with a cup of hot coffee delivered by room service. I was beginning to love this man more and also; I was getting scared. I didn't even have time to think about it when I was with him. It was one beautiful activity to the other: skydiving, surfing, hot stone massage, lunch on a boat cruise, dinner in an exquisite restaurant.

I thought I was learning to see love differently. I didn't even believe in its existence anymore. Men always wanted to be in control around me, but this time was different. I felt free as a flying bird. He never really did anything wrong. All he did was loving me way too much that it hurt. I did everything out of my free will, I felt peace when I was with him. The hugs, the cuddles, the surprises, the scent of his perfume, the scent of incense. The I love you's, the flowers, the secret deliveries of gifts. It wasn't even about the things; it was more about our hearts, and our intentions.

What I remember vividly is that I went back to Toronto after that magical Dubai trip, but he never replied to my texts. He disappeard on me...

I still remember his touch, how he left as soon as I got comfortable in the tiny space he provided for me. I was back to how I started. Lost, thinking of love as a lost cause. I couldn't help but wonder who else was warming his bed, who was giving him the kisses he should be getting from me. Who was in his sheets, wearing his shirt and walking around his house?

I lost the thrill of the city, I lost that sense of direction I thought I had. He made me feel maybe I didn't figure it out after all. He made me feel I was not enough. I felt sadder when I realized I lost Lara, too... She loved Adam, she had feelings for him and I didn't even ask her. And Lara disappeared from my life like I never knew that lovely girl... I never got the closure I was seeking, —may be sometimes things have to get worse before they can get better.

CHAPTER THREE
His Hands

It was I who taught myself how to breathe. I took the time, straining my body against the sun and killing off every single thing which clawed at my chest. It was ridiculous at first because I was not aware I was dying inside. Or maybe I was. Perhaps I knew that both the love I'd felt for Autumn man and Adam had somehow wrecked me and yet I did not want to do anything about it. Still, I needed to breathe; needed to feel alive, joined tightly together with the cosmos. And so with each step I would take down to the place where I worked, I would repeatedly teach myself how to master the art of being alive. For the longest time, Autumn man had been able to lead me and I had followed, willing my heart to be broken down to the right amount of lucidity. Those moments, those flashing memories, were not ones to suddenly leave and disappear. No they were not. With Adam, however, I had opened up my heart and I had kept his clawed out love in it. Letting him go had been the hardest but no longer was I going to let him destroy me with his promising words, his actions and his intoxicating smile. I was going to forget these men regardless because I knew they had not been right for me. And I would throw away the feelings about me and, for once, begin to live.

I was already living my solitary life when I met him. It wasn't a full on kind of life but when I met him, I did not know if I was gradually making a mistake. I did not know what to do with this new found affection. I could not hold it with both hands or tingle it until it felt right in all the places and spots in my body. I could only watch and although it felt good, I sometimes would feel as though my body was going to get burnt with the fire he was bringing out. Aboozar had firm hands and sometimes when he put them on mine, I would tingle and imagine a different world where I wasn't as empty as this. He excited me, thankfully. It had been a while since I found anything mysterious and he was exactly it. He was mysterious but not in a terrible way. The first time I saw him, it was as though I was screaming inwardly to be touched by him. He had held the door for an older lady and I had leaned against the chair in the cafe to watch him. Of course I couldn't do anything about it. I wasn't ready for anything close to love or friendship or any form of relationship and yet this stranger threatened it all. I had learned a lot about giving up on such emotions from men like Autumn man and Adam but this man —this person who did not know I existed— made me feel fragile.

He caught my eye, suddenly and he waved as though he had always known me, as if we were not merely strangers existing in different bodies and different times. I saw that he had the most distant eyes, like he was seeing me and a million other faces all at once and he couldn't quite pinpoint the difference in mine. It was morning and my cup of cold coffee was staring at me but he was the man in my thoughts. For the first time I was not thinking about Autumn man or my need to escape the lingering hold of Adam and his bruised version of intimacy. I was thinking of this stranger with his messy hair and perfect jawline and his weird taste for fashion. When he came to meet me, I was almost convinced he would be the end of me and yet I could never convince my feet to move or to run or to turn away from him. I certainly lost all reasoning when he asked to sit on the chair in front of me. I was after all sitting in a table for two.

"I'm Aboozar," he said matter of fact and I couldn't help but think he was the straight forward type; the kind of man who would be plain and blunt when he wanted to. I did not know if it was what I truly wanted or if I was simply taking the only version of understanding I could scoop up. I did not offer him my name like a menu or a gift card. I said nothing, couldn't quite tell for certain what he truly wanted.

"I caught you staring," he said. "Is it the clothes?" It wasn't really terrible, I told him so and he laughed and he hit the table mildly. He would come to apologise later, over and over again, as if I didn't know the difference between playful fragility and hate.

"I'm Fidan," I said to him.He smiled. "I was thinking we would remain strangers even after all my efforts!" I scowled. "One can hardly classify this as an effort." "Oh?" He arched an eyebrow. "So tell me, Fidan, what do you consider a display of real effort?" Real effort? I did not know that. All my life I had only been surrounded by people who took steps only because it was particularly necessary not because they thought I deserved any of it. I couldn't tell this man what a version of real effort was. I couldn't even tell him why I was scarred from my meticulous flaws. He leaned in and he tipped his head to the side. "The way I see it, we've gone past the idea of strangers, right?" I nodded. He laughed. "You have an accent, Fidan, and I like it. Are you from around here?" I shrugged. He gave me a quick smile. "I understand your hesitancy. I just...I don't...I don't know why or how you pulled me in with your gaze but you did." It was hardly possible to tell if he was wasting both our time because the conversation did not bore me. Instead, it drew me in, pulling me like the rising tides. I would drown and he would be the one luring me in, deeper. Still, for the first time, I couldn't care less if he drowned me. I was not thinking clearly, I knew, and pretty soon this would become a disaster as all the others before him had. But I couldn't pull away. We walked through the park but did not hold hands. We had not gotten up to that point and we both agreed it was too soon, too unbecoming of both our characters. "You don't know me and I don't know you but —" He interrupted me. "But doesn't this just feel so right?" It was, well, it really was but I did not take him up on the offer. To me, he was still a stranger. It was his presence, the general idea that there was someone by my side, which excited me and kept me invested in every word he said and every joke he made. He wasn't funny, Lord, he was barely anything but traditional but he gave me these weird chills. Somehow he walked me to my front porch but by then we each had sweaty palms and brows. "Do you want to come in, perhaps?" I asked him. He shook his head almost immediately. "Thanks, but I think I should get going!" He waved and I waved back and after he was gone, I still stood on the porch, hands by my side, perplexed by his simplicity and gentleness. He was a sharp contrast to Autumn man and Adam but then again, I suppose they all had been gentle and kind at the beginning. Perhaps this was exactly it. I couldn't tell.

A week later, he tapped my shoulders with a smile and I let him hold my hands. We were down in one of the local art galleries but it suddenly felt like we were somewhere private and we had our whole lives passing before our very eyes. "Are you stalking me?" I asked him. He laughed and it was the most honest laughter I had ever heard. "Don't be ridiculous, Fidan." "Do you think I am?" —"Depends," he shrugged. "On what?" He opened my palm and he traced a circle in the middle. Then he looked back at me and I prayed silently to be saved. "I just think you are beautiful, Fidan. And I hate to be cheeky, really, but you really are."

I could feel tingles spinning around my body and the back of my ears burnt badly. Why did I feel so giddy even after all the mistakes of past lovers and past lives?

"Thank you, Aboozar," I said delightfully. He pressed a finger against his forehead.

He walked with me to the street before my house and offered me a smile, one I could not take with one hand. "You do not know me," I said to him. "I know you." —"I mean; it was only forty-five minutes on foot." —"We do not need to spend a lot of time together for me to get to know you," he said. "I see inside you."

I didn't believe in coincidences. He seemed to understand. "I work around here," he eased gently. "That should explain why we keep running into each other." I was not convinced but I was going to let it slide because he looked innocent and normal, and normal was exactly what I needed in my life after Adam. "Can I buy you lunch?" he asked, sliding gently. I was not going to bite but he didn't know that. I answered, "I don't want to intrude." "Intrude on what?" It was not a real question. He raised his hands in surrender and I saw him drag the words out. "You are doing no such thing, please." Then I let him take me to lunch and he took my number and he called that night, his voice throaty and hoarse. —"Do you know that I can count the stars in the night sky?" "How?" — I laughed even though it was not funny in any way. —"I've counted them already in fact," he said. "They are twenty-one billion and forty-three." "Really?" But I did not believe him. "Geeky much?" "Just a little bit too educated," he laughed. "Perhaps it's the real fault." Later when Aboozar learned I was keen on books, he touched my face and held my hands and I felt both safe and warm almost immediately. He had strong hands and it was what I thought about the first time he kissed me. It was soft, gentle but it awakened a fire within me that I could not put out.

I was burning for this man.

One evening, he called. "I want you to read something, Fidan. It's great writing, trust me." I didn't know if I had to trust him but it sounded good hearing it again. I was clinging to anything and anyone who would show me just the slightest bit of emotional attachments and this man was. "Sure," I replied. —"Where's the writing?" —"I'll send it now!" I was done hitting the milk on the stove and pouring it in a mug before his message came through. I sat down on the kitchen floor, first, mug in hand and read through.

I read the words, once, twice, until it was all I could think about. I was delighted that Aboozar had sent this but, in all the different ways, I was consumed by his audacity. This written message had not been composed by him, I knew, but it was fragile and so were the words. I did not understand the gentleness he was showing and wanted to continue to show. I understood nothing but then later,— I tiptoed into my room and read the words again, hoping to see it from a different perspective.

Growing up as a young child sometimes feels like the eruption of awkward laughter; how it slowly moves from the stomach and into the eyes, and how it dips and slithers like a snake.

My mother taught me about values in between small bouts of laughter and love and weaknesses and as I've grown, these values have stretched around my neck. I no longer have to fidget about the rights and wrongs or the ethical standards of classless conversations because my very essence and dignity see past these simple nothings. I believe that to touch the stars, my hands have to be out-stretched. One day, nine million years ago, somebody had stood to look up at the silvery blaze of stars and had day-dreamed about me, arms outstretched still, thinking about life and love and death and the in-between. All of us are like space ships, shuffling about in a bleak moment of truth. I believe in honesty and the simplicity of being sincere; how, in a minute, we could navigate the entire human life if honesty ran through our veins like blood and perhaps a spell of under-standing. My father taught me about honesty. Not with words of mouth, no, but with a careful display of love wrapped around integrity. Building like a war song, he showed me, truly, im-mensely, what it was like for the world t see a little bit of honesty. Someone on the bus showed me the audacity of loving. We were strangers but one hand clasped against mine, brushed away the flimsy fears of what-ifs and maybes. For a while, after-ward, I wondered how my life had changed from that hold and from those eyes that almost looked wounded but had so much love to give. She said to love is the greatest mark of surrender. Isn't the world around your eyes changing? She asked. And she was right. A small show of love was an art of living that made the question of what was infinitely good or bad fall flat. Because what if goodness was a cast of the won-drous play inscribed in the unwritten parts of our lives? The touch and feel of the things within us are a gentle reminder of the works of the world. We could choose, just as we are, to move mountains with the tip of a fingernail and stand in sands, as wa-ter, blue and deep, washed away the quiet ugliness in metaphors.

Our values in life can either propel goodness or a flaw in the workings of our minds. Whatever we hold dear will be a guiding force in how our lives and world are shaped. Slowly, we could learn to finger the edge of the world and love, carelessly, and build the broken things. We could mend the broken with a touch of honesty. If we could push ourselves forward and learn to look at the stars and focus on the simple touch of love and happiness, then the world will be a better place.

It was brutal, vulnerable and well written. It reminded me so much of all I've lost. Tirelessly I have worked my way around people who had a false sense of purpose with me. I remember Autumn man and his hair filled with grey and how I could have learned so much from him if he'd been this willing to guide me. But then Autumn man, as I've come to understand was simply a caricature of the world. He had not been a giver. Now, that I'm older and I can see how mindlessly he'd led me on and I had followed, comely, like a lost child. It had been love although not in that giddy way of loving the sun and the stars and the moon. Aboozar and I had only known for a month but his audacity scared me. I wasn't afraid he would hurt me. No, that was not quite it. I was afraid of putting my heart on the line again. I had learned that putting my heart out with both hands, like a surrender or an anthem of love, was, in other words, a leap into the unknown and I wasn't ready to venture into that again. Under the glow of the fluorescent lights, I scanned the writing again and pretended the writer had envisioned me as he had written this; and that he had ached to trail his fingers along my spine in a pattern of multi colored amusement. When my phone rang, I curled up on the floor, knowing that it was him and he was going to ask about the writings. I took the call in the second ring and lowered my voice until it was nothing more than an awkward plea to take me as I was. "Are you tired? Did I wake you up?" he asked. It was a gentle and thoughtful question, no doubt, but I could not muster the courage to answer him.

"Fidan," he called restlessly.
"I love what you sent," I said to him.

He paused. I could tell my voice had come out forcefully, as if I was angry at him or at someone I couldn't name. "Well, did you?" he asked and I thought he meant something else. Of course I didn't ask him to elaborate or delve into a conversation about unsaid things.

We kept the silence alive for a few more seconds before elasping into small talk. "It isn't Spring yet but I wish it were," I said to him. "Why?" he stumbled over words to say and I could not tell why. He wasn't normally shy or nervous around me. Most of the conversations we'd had had been subtle and generous and I had learned certain things from him. Like the collections of books, he had and which he'd read countless times. He was a true talker but he also had his limits. We hadn't known for too long but I could tell he was the traditional and reserved type. Both Adam and Autumn man had been shallow in the way they folded love like napkins and I had fallen for them because, unlike them, I had always been naive and keen on something as fragile and breathtaking as falling in love. Here, now, with my phone pressed tightly against my ears, I replied, "Spring makes everything look different. I'm happier in Spring." He laughed and it was the most audacious sound I had ever heard. "Well that is new." I examined my chipped fingernails and the closed curtains covered in bunny designs and then took a deep breath. "Do you...do you know where this is going?" He exhaled like he had been holding his breath for that question for far too long. He said, "I want to be more with you, Fidan. I want to love you like the sun loves the sky and I want to marry you."

In the middle of the night, I slipped out of bed and I sat down in the bathroom with the shower on. And I was thinking, miserably, that perhaps if I let the water wash these new emotions and feelings, I would not feel as giddy and excited as I did. It would fail again and again and I wanted it to stop. Thirty minutes later, I knew.

I wanted Aboozar.

***

Before his visit again I made dinner. Aboozar brought icecream as dessert and laughed when he saw how excited I got about it. He leaned against the kitchen door, the way he had learned how to from all the times he had come into my home, and watched me as I sipped white wine.

"I keep looking at you and I don't know how to explain how I feel afterward, Fidan," he said. I arched an eyebrow. "Try, Aboozar," I said. "I really want to know. Explain and I might understand." He opened his mouth to speak but stopped himself and smiled instead. "I'll write about it and show you." I nodded. Once, he had told me about the many times he'd allowed himself dabble in poetry. It was Aboozar who had wrapped me in his steady hands and told me about the times inspiration to write had come to him and he had stood to write. I had not read any of his writings but Aboozar could hold a conversation as easily as he could my hand in a firm and gentle way and so I believed him. He helped to set the table and we sat down and ate. Later, we sank to the kitchen floor with the ice cream and as it melted against my tongue, I thought about how little I knew about this man. Of course I knew his name and how he had first grown up in Turkey and had moved to Toronto years ago. I knew about his love for books and poetry and his joy for works of art. These little details were good enough if I was simply seeking a short relationship that would invariably wither away. But, no, I was in search of something that would quell the anger and hate in my heart. "Aboozar?" I called gently. He looked up at me and his smile dropped. "Are you alright, my dear?"

I nodded quickly before the words fell from my lips. "I want to know more about you." The frown slid off but beneath the facade I saw that he was still tensed. "What do you want to know then?" I could tell that he had not been expecting the question or the way the night would turn out to be after all the laughter and wordless signs of love. Still I did not want to stop. If he wanted to know about me, he too could ask. I was older than I was before and wiser. Yes, that I was and I was not going to lie down, afriad of the outcome of steady questions. "Tell me about your family," I said to him. He swallowed and knitted his fingers together. "They live in Turkey still. I have a younger brother. He's married. My ma and I talk sometimes too." Are you close to both of them?" I asked. Aboozar looked out of breath when I asked him this and for a while, "Is this really important, my love?" I said. ,"I'm not in cotact with my family since I left Turkey, so .."

The silence afterward was awkward, the first since we began talking. "What about your home, Aboozar?" I asked him when we were done with dessert. On the coffee table in the living room, Aboozar's books were piled high. I had not read them all but they did look interesting and sometimes when he would forget them after a rather short visit, I would finger the edges, waiting for the words to somehow come alive. Aboozar's hair was not messy. He had gelled it backward before coming and so when I looked at it, I could not help but admire the sleek style, different from the way I had always known and perceived him to be. "I have a home," he said. "Don't we all?"

And then he laughed but it was nervous and fluctuating and we both knew there was something more. "Right!" I knew that he was trying to avoid the question and it did not sit too well with someone like me. Aboozar leaned against the wall and he folded his arms over his chest. His furrowed brows told me he was thinking and would soon come up with a suitable explanation for his flaws.

The silence slowly began to turn awkward before he turned to look at me. "Do you really want to know?" He bit down hard against his lower lips and I thought he would back out any chance he got. I nodded. "Home was a skeletal mask of watercolors and the sound of an eight record player skipping forgotten tunes. It was a place sandwiched between an oak tree and a garden where sunlight spilled through in small gaps like the in between of a smoker's tooth. It was beautiful —that small house with the faded paint and creaky stairs— and I lived there for a thousand years. I say thousand years to mean the convergence of every sad and happy memory all meeting in a multi colored string and I mean it. "Adelaide used to come visit sometimes in the summer. He was my best friend but he was also my cousin. His body used to smell like the sands in a beach but his somewhat tanned skin did not look natural. I read somewhere we could pretend to exist in a miniature universe while our bodies learned to capture the nothingness of reality. Often, when I stared at my cousin I would think about that lesson, hanging above our heads like something omnipresent and I would smile, burning and suffocating with the things I couldn't quite say. He had a tattoo of a whippoorwill on his left arm and one day, he said to me, "We grow out of our skins, you know," his voice was low and shaky like an amateur beat of an ukulele but his eyes bore down hard against my cheeks. "One day this bird on my arm is going to disappear. Look at it any way you want but the way I see it; it's going to either die or fly away." "I was thirteen then and the crippling sensation of being told this faded after months. He was a lot older and when he started to grow out of his skin, I knew. I was maybe almost seventeen when he kissed me. It was small, like the beginning of a tap dance, but afterward it grew with a force even I couldn't keep up." I did not know what to tell him. This slow reveal of his childhood took me by surprise. I could not tell for certain if I wanted him to stop or continue to tell me about his cousin and the kiss and the fleeting moment of self awareness afterward. "Do you think I am a confused person?" He asked me. I shrugged but then thought otherwise. "I believe that you have a good heart." He smiled and he reached for my hand. He squeezed gently and I could feel myself floating away. "I don't talk to him anymore. But sometimes I wonder about our exploration when we are younger; how often, at childhood and young adulthood, we feel rebel until...well, we aren't. Do you understand, Fidan?"

I understood everything because I had been just that. I had thought I was solid before Autumn man and Adam but later I had discovered, with their sickening help that I was nothing and I had to accept it. Aboozar did not need to explain further. I had been in different places too.

"Of course I understand," I said to him.

He reached over and he cupped my face in his open palm as gently and as stable as he could. I could not breath under his gaze and as close as he was, I imagined he was far away, the way the people I have ever loved were. I wanted to push Aboozar away now but as my hands touched his body, cold fear seeped into my bones and a lingering question arose from within me: for what if I pushed him away and the loneliness and depression returned? How would I be able to live?

"Kiss me," I whispered.

It was the first time that I asked for it before someone took from me, I felt incredibly alive suddenly. This man was both venerable and strong, a combination I had ached for for far too long. Of course it was here now and I wanted to scream at the world. His lips brushed mine first, grazing me softly before fully taking me in. It was to be the highest moment of passion where, together, we combined our flaws and our perfection and they became like fireballs. His lips on mine tasted like cherry, leaving me in a dizzy awe. His hands covered my face, driving the panic away and keeping me grounded and I fell in with him, decidedly, the way the sun belonged to the sky. There was indeed a throbbing so intense and carnivorous where his lips had been. His fingers grazed my skin lightly.

"I can open up to you, Fidan, without being afraid."
"I suppose the same goes for both of us," I said, laughter in between my teeth. He did not know, yet, how flawed I was and how far away I was from home. He did not know about the silly maneuverings my heart had done for the sole purpose of being touched

by him. He shuffled his feet and ran a hand through his hair until it was all but messy. Aboozar avoided my gaze like it was the face of a new and strange woman and he wanted to be far away suddenly. I could not tell if this feeling about us made me happy or indifferent.

"Do you want to stay over?" I asked him after a while.

He shook his head quickly. "I couldn't possibly impose."

"You aren't, really," I said to him.

He hesitated and I could see he was thinking. He licked his lower lip and then looked at me. "You are ... you are ...so attractive..."

I didn't know what to do. Aboozar looked at me like no one ever had, not like the manipulative way Adam did or the controlling way Autumn-man handled me. Aboozar was different, but I'd been burned too many times by men who seemed too exotic and too beautiful for words. I decided there and then that I was going to throw caution to the wind and just have that night to myself. Maybe I was being selfish or whatever, but I didn't want to be anything else, not while I could have the world I wanted on a platter of gold. Of course, there'd be mistakes but I was past caring.

Adam taught me that if I wanted anything, I just had to stretch my hands to get it. The process didn't matter, only the result did. And, I wanted Aboozar. I wanted him in a way that frightened even me. I wanted to take it slow at first, but I didn't care anymore. Why should I? Everyone I wanted was either a douche or something close to it. Manipulators on every front. No, that wasn't the kind of life I wanted to live, scared of my own shadow. I wanted to be lord over my own life, knowing that everything I did was done because I wanted to. Adam was a lot of things and most of them destroyed me more than I could say. But then, I learnt. To play the mad game, caution was not necessary.

Autumn man showed me a side of life that I never understood, seeing as he was older and with way more experience. He played me like a fiddle, and I danced to the tune. He was adept at it. A maestro even. And no matter how much I hated what he turned me into, I couldn't deny that with him, I could let down my hair because he wanted to do everything for me. He wanted to control my very existence. I hated that but seeing from his viewpoint, he was a powerful man who wasn't used to not getting his way. He made nonsense of our time together and at a point, I hated my own self. But now...

Aboozar didn't have to pretend, I could see his need clearly in his eyes. He didn't have to hide. What he felt, he wore on his arm like a sleeve. Maybe that would have been a turn-off for some women but that wasn't the case with me. With my experience with men, I chose Aboozar because I didn't have to second guess myself with him, he made me feel more of myself than I'd ever felt ordinarily. That was no small mercy. So, I decided to show him my appreciation in one way I've never failed at.

I pushed him to the chair, slowly moving my hips to a slow music I put on the stereo. I needed him to be comfortable, and I needed to take charge. Maybe then I'd get over my trauma and move forward, knowing that I did the best I could and prevailed. I came closer to him and straddled him, a wicked grin on my face. I was enjoying myself. I couldn't think of a time when I enjoyed myself the way I did then, it was nothing short of magical. I wanted to relish every single second of it and whatever happened after then, I wasn't going to saddle myself with regret of any kind. I chose this and because of that, I was going to move forward.

"Let me take care of you..." I managed to say as he swallowed, eyes transfixed on my face. The feral look in his eyes set me afire and before long, I wanted him to take me there and then. But, no. That wasn't how I moved. I needed to be coy, sly, and whatever else. I intended to do whatever I wanted and nothing on earth was going to stop me. I'd been sheltered for too long by men who'd rather bed a thousand women just to prove their superiority. I was done with worrying about whatever they did. It was time to worry about myself and what I wanted. And I wanted Aboozar. I was going to take total control and I was going to love every step.

"Can I touch you?" He asked, eyes glazed over with need. I could feel the tent in his shorts, and I smiled again. He was perfect for my experiment. He was willing too and maybe he was going to help me get over everything. Then, I could be what I wanted to be, with no apologies, and no questions asked. The sex

I wanted was to be a cleansing, healing from everything I'd experienced from Autumn man and Adam. It was going to save me, even from myself. Maybe I was using Aboozar for my own nefarious reasons, but I wasn't going to apologize, no. I was going to take the bull by the horn and confront it once and for all.

"No. You can't. I'll do the touching. Just focus on feeling. You'll touch me when I want you to. Is that understood?" I said, stopping momentarily. He nodded slowly and I placed a kiss on his lips, extended and full of the promise of what I could do to him later on. I was ready to go wild, and I wouldn't let anyone take that from me, not even Aboozar himself. This was my time to shine, my time to do whatever. I missed Aboozar, my tongue searching his mouth as his tongue rose up to meet mine. I didn't shy away, I crashed my lips onto his, making him gasp for air. Then, I stopped. The feeling was heady, knowing how much I could casually control. I didn't want the feeling to stop, I didn't want to return to the woman I was; grossly insecure. No, that wasn't the woman I wanted to be. I was going to be bold, to take what I wanted. This was me and I was not going to apologize for that. Not to anyone.

I placed my hand on his chest, having discarded the top clothes he wore. I didn't have time for subtlety. I wasn't even bothered to explain the frenzy with which I attacked his body. I used my fingers to pinch his nipples and he groaned in pleasure. The sound was like music to my ears, I didn't want it to stop. I pinched his nipples again and just when he thought that was all I wanted to do, I surprised him by putting my head down and sucking one of his nipples, making him let air out through gritted teeth along with a groan. He was sensitive, more than I expected. I brought out a tongue and licked his tiny nipples, making him hold onto whatever he could. But, I wasn't done, not by a long shot.

I pinched one nipple and sucked on the other and he relinquished control to me completely. I felt powerful, more powerful than I'd ever felt before. I had him at my grasp, in the palms of my hand. I could do whatever I wanted, and the possibilities were making my head woozy. I couldn't believe how much I was affecting him almost casually. That emboldened me even more and I trailed a tongue down to his abdomen. He was cleanly shaved so there was no hair for me to play with. It was such a shame though, I always wondered what the combination would be like…

But I couldn't be a spoilsport, so I traced a tongue past his abdomen. I was burning from deep within, not believing how much fun could be had from being totally in control. It was a heady feeling, like getting drunk on exotic wine and having deep conversations into the night. I was entranced, not wanting all of it to end. Because then… then I'd return to Fidan, the woman who didn't know what she wanted from life. But, no more of that. I needed to enjoy myself without thoughts of the past creeping up on me.

I pulled down his trousers and the briefs followed. I didn't have the time to dilly-dally. No. I wanted to do something wild and unconventional. I needed Aboozar to feel the way I felt, to feel what I wanted to do to him. I could feel the wetness pooling between my legs, but I pointedly ignored it. It wasn't time for my pleasure yet. I was going to have as much fun as I wanted before then. His manhood sprang out and bobbed a few times as though excited to see me. I placed one of my fingers on the tip and Aboozar let out a whoosh of air through his mouth and gritted teeth. He was making me feel even more powerful as time went on and I got even bolder, taking his length in my hands, and wrapping my fingers around it.

"I'm going to do something..." I said with a sly smile and before he could ask what I meant, I used my mouth to cover his manhood, making him jerk with pleasure. I used my other finger to trace a line down his manhood while my mouth adjusted to the intrusive feel of his manhood in my mouth. Then, I began to move my mouth. I knew that what I was doing was technically torture but I didn't care, I wanted to feel what total control felt like. What it meant. And what a ride that was.

Aboozar was speaking words I didn't understand or even tried to. All I knew was that my mouth was making him speak in tongues. My confidence shot through the roof. But then, who could blame me? I never took liberties with a male body before. Content to let the men lead, I did whatever they asked me to, no questions asked. Aboozar gave me a present, even though he didn't know it yet. I decided not to tell him, since there was no point to that. I decided to show him. To show him just how much I appreciated that. Although he wouldn't have known, since he was on cloud 9. My tongue moved along with my lips, sucking on his length and letting my tongue dance around it. He was groaning and moaning, making me smile through what I was doing. I never imagined that I could have as much fun as I did without consequences. After then, I let my mouth do the talking on his length. I sucked, fondled, and kissed. Aboozar didn't act like someone who'd had that done to him before, so I guessed that I was doing him a service. My fingers fondled the balls underneath and he was lost by then. Whenever I noticed that he was about to orgasm, I stopped. Then, I let him simmer for a minute or two. After that, I resumed what I was doing. He was lost in a world of my own choosing, and nothing was going to make me relinquish authority. Not even on my life.

But then, I was turned on enough to have my wetness drip down the side of my thighs. I couldn't focus on him too much anymore, my body needed care and attention too and somehow, it was as though he knew. He took a few moments before he stood up and looking at me square in the eyes, he said,

"Allow me to treat you with the same care you've treated me." I could hear the double entrendè but I didn't say a word. I could feel myself clamming up, thoughts of the past that equated to trauma showing up in my vision. I almost bolted out of the house then, to a place, any place. But then, Aboozar looked at me. Not flippantly, no. Never flippantly. He looked at me, really looked at me and I felt my walls melting down to rubble.

"I won't hurt you, Fidan. Do you trust me?" He asked. It was my time to nod. He placed his hands gingerly on my thighs and I felt self-conscious almost suddenly. But then, he calmed me down and looked at me again. This time, he made sure my eyes met his and stayed there for a while. I didn't understand, maybe I didn't want to. So, he put all of it into words I could understand.

"Do you trust me, Fidan? Do you trust me not to harm you in any way? Just say the word and I'll stop. The reins lie in your hands. Don't forget that." Aboozar said, opening me up to new possibilities, new adventures. I felt like taking control was the only way but what if I could take control without being in control? I didn't think there was anything else that came close to that and honestly, I wasn't sure I wanted to know anything else. Aboozar stared at me, and he really saw me, not the brave front I often projected or the weakling beneath. No, this was the real me, the one standing tall even with flaws enough to paint a three storey building.

"I trust you, Aboozar. I trust you with my body and mind." I said and the smile he sent my way melted my heart all of a sudden. I didn't know if I wanted to cry but I suspected so. But I kept everything in, not wanting to betray my feelings. Aboozar was kind, he listened to me and didn't try to make me feel any less than I was. That was all I wanted, to have a semblance of control. Maybe not all of it but enough to make my sexual life feel like it was mine and not done at the whims of anybody else.

Aboozar didn't say any words after that, he took his time to unclad me, unraveling me like one of the best presents he'd ever gotten. I was feeling self-conscious but he didn't let it linger, not for long. I was at his mercy, and he wanted to show me that it wasn't a bad thing or something to be shied away from, never like that. Aboozar wanted to teach me from scratch. Even though his manhood was pulsing in front of me, he didn't look like he cared. He wanted to take care of me, and he said it in more words than one. I was head over heels, but I felt like it was too soon to give him my heart after giving him my body. It didn't seem right somehow, so I suppressed the feeling, not letting it see the light of day. It was clamped down on, until whenever I was ready.

He was good with his hands, often asking me questions at interval that warmed my heart considerably. The questions might have seemed flippant to some but to me, they meant the entire world and I wasn't sure he even knew how much those questions elicited in me.

"How do you feel? Do you want me to stop? To go slower? Maybe faster?" He asked those questions at interval, ignoring his very obvious needs for mine. His self-control stunned me. I'd heard that men were animals or beasts. So many adjectives that Aboozar disproved just with the way he handled me. He did all of it with care, making tears leak out of my eyes unbidden. He kissed the tears, and kissed me softly on the lips, making me taste the salty tang that the taste of tears came with.

"I won't hurt you; I promise." He said over and over again, reassuring me with every breath. I was losing myself to him and this time, I wasn't scared. There was no iota of fear within me as at then, knowing that he was with me. I felt powerful, more powerful than I'd ever felt with anybody else. He wanted me, he made it clear. He didn't mince words, but he made me choose. He didn't impose his will on me but let me decide. In a way, I controlled his actions. I'd never imagined that such a thing existed. Or maybe I didn't think I was worthy of it. I didn't think I was worthy of a lot of things and somehow, Aboozar corrected my misconception. He made me see the things I remained resolutely blind to because of the men I've been with and the kind of mindset I had while growing up.

"Never let anybody tell you that you don't count. You do. Even more, than you know. You're special and you're beautiful. Don't forget how beautiful you are." Aboozar said in between kisses at the space between my legs. I covered my face, but I wasn't self-conscious because he made me feel shy or made me feel a certain way, not at all. I was self-conscious because of the cacophony of emotions swirling within me. It was heady, I couldn't even believe such clashes of beautiful feelings existed.

He kissed me down there, reassuring me as he did. I grabbed his head, throwing my shame and shyness to the wind. I wasn't going to miss out on the best experience of my life because of my hang-ups about certain things. No, I couldn't do that to myself. I wanted him to see how much I wanted him, so I said it as plainly as I could, hoping he wouldn't think me forward or anything close to that.

"I want you inside of me. And I want that now Aboozar." I said, knowing that I was walking uncharted territories, but I didn't care. For the first time, I didn't second guess myself, or try to make accommodations for my words. I just said them as they came to me and didn't even flinch. No, I wasn't going to. I needed to embrace myself.

"As you wish," Aboozar said, making me smile as he slowly plunged himself inside of me. He was slow at first, his length filling me with wonder. Somehow, it increased in length and width as it entered inside of me. I could feel myself stretching to accommodate him. I grabbed his face and kissed him full on the face as he plunged into me even faster and I moved my hips in sync with his, creating a beautiful symphony. When I felt my orgasm come, I used my legs to clamp him down, as we screamed together, his hips moving faster and mine doing the same. I lost the sense of time and space, the sense of right or wrong. I didn't know where I was or what I was doing but I knew for sure that I was getting somewhere.

Then, I screamed out as my orgasm wracked through me, while he came almost immediately. We screamed in one accord, our voices melding and becoming one as the feeling of pleasure unlike any other consumed us whole. This time, I held on to him like the sole lifeline of a sinking ship, scared to let go. That was how I was when I passed out.

***

It was raining when his alarm rang and I felt him rise from the bed. He had the sheets wrapped around his body. I opened my eyes just a little bit to stare at the man that I now loved with the whole of my heart. He wiped the sweat from his forehead with the back of his hand and opened the window then he swallowed the smell of fresh damp rain with all his being.

Calm down. Calm down ... he had a dream ... like a monk who performs a ritual. I whispered incomprehensible words under my breath and covered my half-naked body with my black silky hair. He closed the window. Then he stepped quietly to the grate to put some firewood in the fireplace. He got up from the fireplace. He went in front of the mirror and put his hand on his wavy hair. His wheat skin was shining. A few handfuls of cold water hit him in the face ....
He took a shawl from the wardrope wrapped it around his neck. He put on his long black leather boots, tucked a key and a few sheets of paper in his emerald coat pocket, and left the house.

I fell back asleep. Perhaps it had all been a dream. I felt safe in his bed. It had been an hour since the rain had given way to a velvety snowfall. However, the weather was not cold. His cheeks were flushed. He had a strange feeling. He entered the castle cafe, the only place where he could find peace. Its dark brown tables, its low ceiling, the candles flickering in the corner, and the smell of coffee mingled with a martini that caressed your breath and plunged its guests into the ecstasy of its antiquity came to meet him. Or maybe time had lost its meaning. He used to sit at a small table and look out of the empty chair facing the outside of the cafe. Now, he wanted to make things right but he also needed to think. He took his seat close to the window and started. No faces could be seen from behind the window; There were only umbrellas and scarves. His heart rubbed. Perhaps it was time he became fully honest. He did not come back home that night. I called him but when he refused to take my calls, I took my things and left his key by the pot. It was evening when he came to meet me in my house. He was standing there by the door when I pulled it open. Aboozar stared at me with keen eyes, waiting and expecting me to turn him away. It broke my heart to see him there, alone and wrecked but I knew that it would be a terrible thing to let him in. It wasn't about him, really. It was for me. I could not hold him or pull him closer for fear of being burnt alive. I could not grab him with both hands and surrender myself the way he wanted and so turning him away seemed like the only choice I now had. He had a gift bag in his right hand and another in his left. These, he raised towards me like a sacrifice, as if, perhaps, he was laying down his hopes for me to touch. "Please...?" He looked past my shoulders. The lights in the kitchen fluctuated and dimmed and he closed his eyes momentarily. "Just let me in, Fidan, please. We need to talk about everything."

Talking about all the times my impulsive behaviour had roped onto the surface of our relationship did not, in any way rise to the surface. At the moment, there was only one thing to do: let me in. Still, my hands would not let go of the door or step aside for him to enter. It was as if I was complete at this moment without his steady hands or lingering gaze and I knew that this was simply a mirage and that under the facade I was empty but I did not move. "Let me in," he said again and this time, his voice was more firm, commanding. "We need to talk. It's important." I sighed deeply before allowing him in.

When he stepped in, I closed the door but did not move away from it. He turned around to meet my eyes. He was here now and he had something to discuss and his eyes looked torn as if he had been unable to sleep. "What do you want to talk about that's so import-ant?" I asked him, throwing the words at his silence. He passed me the gift bags and for fear that I would hate his gifts, I placed them on the dining room table. "Can we sit first?" he asked. I followed him to the liv-ing room and he sat on the chair while he sat down on the floor. Music was playing softly in the background. He brought a book out and he showed it to me. "I wrote this," he said. "It's a collection of poems dedicated to you." "That's...wonderful," I breathed cheaply. It was good to hear these words from him; intoxicating to listen to how his lips would curl around the remnants of my name and pride but it was also excruciatingly painful. Like how he would say a mil-lion about me and this relationship and I would not understand a thing.

Aboozar opened the book to the first page where the dedication sat idly. He read it out and he smiled up at me. I returned the smile, wider, because I did not know of anything else. When he read the first poem for me, he smiled again like a proud father and

I thought about Istanbul for the first time in years. I was thinking about home surrounded by trees and my mother desperately covering up her hair and body and shame. I thought about the streets and the money and all the times I had ended up at the embassy with nothing but pocketful of regrets. Then, I thought about Autumn man and how he could easily have been a mentor but had taken and taken and how Adam had stained his teeth with another girl's lips. And I knew that I couldn't handle it again."What did you want to talk about?" I asked again.Aboozar's smile dropped and he placed the book on the coffee table. He would forget it here, I thought to myself.

"I..." He stopped and glanced up at me. "Please forgive me, Fidan, I have not been fully honest with you."

When he said that, I thought about how lonely it would be tonight and how I would begin to hate him although how that was possible was beyond me. I loved Aboozar. I wanted him. I ached for him. I could never hate him and yet when he said those words, it was all I could think about.

"What?" I asked.

He stood up and he looked at me. "I am... married."

Laughter erupted from within my throat. It was impossible. This was perhaps a joke but Aboozar looked serious and I could not tell what was going on in his head.

"That's crazy," I blurted out. "You couldn't possibly

be married, right?"

He shook his head. "I don't know how else to tell you but I could not keep lying to your face." I glanced down at the floor and closed my mind from thinking. I did not want to think. I did not want to feel a thing.

"What about now? — You're lying to me!" I said. My voice had risen but I did not care. "We aren't together anymore," he said. "I want to divorce her and be with you fully but I can't do that if you don't know the truth."

There was no truth to be spoken now, only lies. I wanted him gone. —"Get out," I said to him. Aboozar looked at me with his eyes and for a second I got lost in them like I had fallen into the ocean.

He said, "Please do not do this, Fidan. I love you."

There was no love and I was seeing it now. I told him and he groaned and shuffled his feet. "We could work around this, please," he said.

I said no.

Maybe he was running away too. We wanted to take refuge in each other, unaware that we had just piled up a lot of holes inside us on another head and named it love!

When love promised the end of loneliness, we were greedy.

I did not tell him that I did not live, I died! He did

not know that I was thirsty to run away from myself and instead shouted that I was running away from people and that the glorious name of freedom had fallen on my loneliness. And I will not find a way to escape from freedom to build this ruin of loneliness. Aboozar's words were scattered in the air, and since I did not want the vacuum of life to take over, he snatched his words in the air and kept them to himself. He thought he wanted to make a pillar out of his words for life, but they smoked and went to the same air. Aboozar was a compassionate ruthless man I knew that now.

I wanted to start the journey of love when that one-sentence story of my life came to me again, "Raw imagination string! I wanted to attach his story to the empty story of my life so that I could bear the image of my loneliness in the mirror. He said nothing and I knew it wasn't some-thing he could easily explain in words.— And then, in endless silence, his eyes stared into the distance. He seemed to be lost, but as far as he told me he had lost nothing but himself. Aboozar did not know that love needed words; Even the words that smoke and go up in the air. It may be possible to enjoy the wordless feeling for a short time, but one brings little. This damn heart wants its hands; Consecutive assurances and eye-to-eye stitching. The happiness that I had experienced was not hap-piness, it was waiting for happiness. His bright heart sucked he blood out of my life and so I knew it was time to let him go.

CHAPTER FOUR
Inside Out

I leaned back against my chair and shuffled my feet. There wasn't a single sound disrupting the whirring of the ceiling fan overhead but I pretended there was. My therapist was no longer staring. She had her right arm pressed down to her side. The other was against her eyes, and she was quiet. I could tell she was thinking. I had shared too much with her, I knew, but I could not stop. Not yet. Not now.

I needed her to know about the insecurites I had faced as I had been submerged in ice. I wanted her to know about the tingling sensation of loving someone too much, too evenly, and dying because of it every single time. I wanted her to know everything but this pause to the conversation stopped me Then she looked at me with an arched eyebrow and I worried she was thinking too much. She twirled her pen in her left hand and frantically, I sought to remember how she had gotten it. She had told me the story before; how he'd body had sank deeper into the reflective feeling of being shown just the right amount of love. She'd said the story of how she'd been gifted the pen which had invariably become her favorite for therapy sessions on my second day and I had observed the excited way she had said so. Later, it had reminded me of the giddy way I used to feel all the time with Autumn man and Adam.

She pursed her lips, curled it as though there were a million words she couldn't say but which were bubbling to the surface. I stared at her hair instead, admiring the straightness of the blonde. I could tell she'd spent so much time combing through it, taking out the tangles from it and measuring it with the tip of her nails. In her office I did not feel so small but there was a mechanical dependency to the words that came out of my mouth to fill up the room. She did not make me feel powerless and ridiculous but sometimes I envied the way she looked sane and the calculated way she eased into every conversation.

May was her name but she told me I could call her anything I wish. I called her May regardless. "Do you want tea?" she asked suddenly. I nodded, briefly and she stood and she rang a bell. When tea was brought in, she passed me a cup and then took hers. "Take some biscuits too," she said, urging me in the gentlest way; the way she usually did when I would burst out crying. Like when I told her about Autumn man and the night he'd stood me up. "He could have been busy, the way he said it," she had said. "No, don't say that," I said almost screaming. "He hurt me."

I reached over and took one and placed it neatly on my tongue. It tasted like strawberries and I wanted it to stay so. The tea was just as I liked which was concerning because I'd never accepted her invitation for tea and biscuits before. I sipped dutifully from the cup and thereafter placed it back on the small coffee table by my sofa. The office was not small but it often felt so. Her mahogany desk and chair sat mildly at the corner, close to the window. From there, I could see the sun and could hear the sounds of passing cars. There was a plant on the table too. I remembered Peace Lily and its smell and then I remembered leaving it all behind. The floor was covered in a beautiful rug. "It's from Persia," she said the first time I had observed it in words. "My brother bought it when he went on a visit. Don't you like it?" I had nodded, afraid to tell hermy fears lurking behind every conversation and leaking into every ounce of self respect I had left. "What did you like most about Autumn man?" May now asked. I shrugged. She sipped from her cup and placed it back down. "You're here to talk and grow and I'm here to help you."

I could feel her tenacious spirit from where I sat and it was breathtakingly surreal. Never before had I felt something so kind and honest and beautiful and seeing it now in the body of some other human made me re think my entire existence. For what if I'd never been made into this selfish being because of the decisions I had let my mind delve into? Or, hypothetically, what if I had been made into this pathetic version of Fidan because I had let my body and mind fall for men who took and took from me and yet offered love like it was privilege; like I had to work my bones off to feel the slightest hint of love and devotion and appreciation. "So tell me..." May leaned forward. I took in whiffs of her perfume. It was heavy against her body and as I took it in, I wanted to rub my hands against my chest. There was no unique similarity between both the smell of her expensive perfume or my aching need to wrap my hands across my neck like in a surrender but I was older now. I was all the older but not wiser. As a forty-two-year-old woman, one would expect me to be wise and a little kept but I wasn't. I wasn't exactly carefree either and it was this imbalance that wrecked me.

"Let's talk about Autumn man first," she said. "Are you okay talking about him?" I frowned. For two sessions, I'd told her all about Autumn man and Adam, portraying them as people who were still present within me and in the world. I had told her about Aboozar and she had made a joke about my romantic acceptance of men with their names starting as A... Yet here she was asking me if I was comfortable talking about him or answering questions about them. If I wasn't I wouldn't even be in here with her. "What do you want to know?" I asked her. She sipped her tea again but did not take a biscuit from the plate. When she kept the cup down, I saw that she looked younger and my eyes widened in disbelief. Surely she was older. I didn't ask her and she didn't say. She shrugged, then she said, "Do you perhaps miss him sometimes?" — "No—"

"Listen, Fidan," she whispered calmly, the way one would do to a growing child. —"I want you to think deeply about this. You stayed with that man for years and for a long time you loved him." I interrupted her almost immediately she said those words. "I did not love him. I know now." "You say that now because you're older, more matured and you can think clearly," she said. "But back then you were younger and you called whatever passed between both of you love." I said nothing because she was almost right. "Now tell me, Fidan, do you sometimes miss him?"

I whispered his name to feel his presence and at once I felt a touch on my neck and it was burning and burning and lifting me off my feet to the rug. I pushed both knees together, waiting, preparing for the final sensation of utmost dread.

"Stop it, Fidan!"

I heard a voice but I could not put a face to it. I closed my eyes for a second and I saw myself in his apartment, visiting it for the thousand time in my mind. It was so long ago I saw him or heard about him but as I stood in the threshold, he stepped away from the shadows and he took me into the living room. My picture was hung on the wall. There was a blue and white vase on a low stool by the door to the kitchen. The walls had changed its color from white to a dull kind of yellow. The place smelt of white wine and cheese and garlic. He was cooking, and I wondered if rice was still his favorite or he'd moved on, like me. "Don't fall back in your head, Fidan!" I heard the voice again and slowly, the face of a stranger was appearing before me. Autumn man was older now and his teeth were no longer white. He smelt different too; the cold smell of a pocket of wasted years pressed firmly against his skin like a tattoo. I should have gotten one. "Dance with me," he said. —"But there's no music," I whispered. He kissed my fingers and my cheeks and my nose. "Dance with me."

I nodded, took his hands and moved my feet. Except we weren't dancing. Autumn man did not move. A small smile crept up his lips, lifting up the corners of his mouth in a breathless attack. His eyes were no longer blue or brown or green. They were empty and cold and black. Frightened, I moved away from him, running back towards the door and away from his reach. This man caught me by the hair and he grabbed fistfuls, jerking me back towards his body. Someone was laughing and I was drowning and I couldn't make a face. "Stop it, Fidan!" — My eyes opened and my therapist hands was joined to mine. She had a concerned expression but I didn't want to wipe it away because I wasn't okay. I couldn't be okay. "It's going to be fine," she whispered in a most caring voice. She sounded like the very version I would have wanted my mother to sound and at once, she wasn't older or younger to me. She was May and she was my therapist.

I touched my cheeks. It was wet and cold. I didn't know that I had been crying but when my hands revealed the truth my mouth couldn't say, I closed my eyes again.

"Do you need help standing?" I opened them again and blinked back tears. "What?" She repeated the question. "Do you want me to help you get on your feet?" I nodded. She placed one hand over my shoulder and lifted me up and I curled up on the sofa, clutching my wrist. She sat back on her chair and drank the last of her tea. "It's grown cold," she said, laughter in her eyes. Her lips trembled. She didn't say anything about the trance or how I had been crying and clutching fistful of my hair. She simply made a joke about her tea.

I drove home, alone. In my kitchen, I leaned against the ceramic counter top and counted how many times I had relapsed emotionally, charging at myself for all the men I had loved since Istanbul. In Toronto, there wasn't much time to think about past lovers and truthfully, I didn't want to think. Still, I would relapse and the nightmares would come, daringly, until I would withdraww from work and from everyone. It was probably the reason I had agreed to see a therapist. I tiptoed to the window and I pressed my face against the glass, pretending I was a butterfly flying about like a dancing astronaut. It made no sense to me but it afforded me the chance to be a certain kind of way and i could breathe and stand and understand little of nothing. From the kitchen I made my way to my room and settled clumsily against the edge of the bed. The room was mine and I had lived here for years already but suddenly it felt alien to me and I couldn't tell what I hated most about the place. It could not have been the curtains, yellow and dusty, held firmly by a single rope nor could it have been the sheets stacked neatly by the bed. No, it was me and I could not do anything about it. That made me wonder about everything I had said and every mistake I had made, tactfully turning it in my head to make sense of it all. I walked into the bathroom, turned on the shower head and let the water run down my skin. It was much later that I discovered I was still wearing my clothes and socks. It came as a shock so that I pulled away almost immediately and dragged myself back to the room. I took the clothes oft, dumped them in a pile and touched the wall. It was stable and real and I didn't know if what I truly needed was something to break. It would have been an almost remarkable experience if it was happening outside of my body or if I was floating, mildly betraying gravity and it's hold on my skin. But it wasn't. It was a fright, chilling to the bones, to discover I was losing myself and my mind in the relative absurdity of my heart. I did not sleep. I took my phone and I dialled my sister's number. It rang and then stopped. I tried again. She didn't take the call. I kept the phone back down and sat on the floor with my back against the wall. I was still naked and broken. I thought about my sister, dutifully hating me for breaking the way sunflowers and lilies did. Would she ever want to speak to me? Of course I was broken. It had happened not because I wanted it to but because there had been no other way out. What was I to do anyway? I had helped myself in any case, Lord knows that. I had tried and tried and although it wasn't of much help these days, it was still a step.

My therapist opened the door to her office at the next session. I saw that she was wearing a blouse and a skirt and had mascara made perfect by her beautiful eyes. It was the first thing I would come to notice about her and the place. She let me sit on the purple sofa. It would come to be my favorite in her office. Then she sat opposite, in a low chair. The place was unusually dark but I could still make out ripples of self awareness lodged in my chest. She crossed her legs by the ankle and produced a note pad and her favorite pen. "Hi," she breathed. "How are you, Fidan?" I shrugged. "I don't know, May." She nodded and adjusted her glasses. She wasn't a glasses type, I could tell, but it suddenly looked good on her. I did not tell her about it though but I reckoned she could guess so. "You didn't go to work today," she observed. She twirled her pen. I couldn't tell what she was thinking. "And then you scheduled today's session earlier than usual. Are you alright?" She was right. "I couldn't sleep," I said to her. "I tried calling my sister but she wouldn't take the calls and I couldn't sleep." "What about work?" I shrugged. She said, "You know, Fidan, sometimes when I look at you, I imagine a myriad of questions running through your mind. You want to know why you don't feel happy or why you are the way you are, I know, but please answer me honestly. How are you?" I thought about it for a long time. In the silence, she watched me and I watched her. I wasn't seeing her but I wasn't seeing anybody in particular. I was simply seated atop her sofa, with my hands knitted in front of me and my mind wavering. How did she know?

She wanted honesty and I wanted, no needed to be rid of the pain deep in my head. So I did the one thing she asked of me. I made some honest statement. I said, "I'm fine."

"Oh okay, Fidan," she whispered. I sniffed. Don't cry, don't cry, don't cry, please!

"Do you want to say something else?"

She was gentle with her words. "When I say I am fine, I mean that when I thought about slitting my wrist two nights ago, I did not. And when I thought about the familiarity of drowning and how beautiful death would feel like pressed against my skin, I did not jump into an ocean."

May nodded and wrote something in her book.

"So when I tell you that I'm fine, that's what I mean."

"That you could have killed yourself but you didn't?" May voiced the words out tentatively.

I played with my hair and shuffled my feet. "That's what I mean, yes."

"I understand," she said and she looked like she did.

"What got me here?" I asked her after a while. "I was free before, you know, but now..."

"What about now?"

"I —i don't know," she said. "I don't even know what freedom means now."

May placed her book and pen on the small table and she clasped her hands together. "I'll tell you what freedom is, Fidan," she said. "Freedom is not that you can do whatever you like, freedom means you do not have to do what you do not like."

That made a lot of sense to me but it still did not remove the anger in my head or the feeling of being ridiculous despite it all.

"I have something to give you, Fidan," she said and stood.

I wondered what it was she wanted to gift to me and then I asked myself if, truly, I'd want to be given such a gift. If it was a pen, I'd use it to write down the things I didn't want the world to know, just as I used to do when I was still with Autumn man. If it was tea and biscuits again, I would say no as politely as I could. She came back with a book and instictively I groaned. It wasn't loud but it was enough for her to smile in pity. I had a growing pile of books at home that I was never going to read and now she was adding this to it without my consent. It bothered me because I did not want to read. I wanted to be... saved.

"It's going to help you, **Fidan**," she said.

I took the book from her. Then she sat down and she picked up her notepad and pen again. "The book in your hand is the experience of a woman who one day was a little girl," she said. "Yes, small. Not because of height and slate. Because one hundred and seventy cents and 5 kilos is not considered small by the standards of measurement in these days of the world." I said nothing. I simply fingered the book with my nails, half listening to her.

She continued, "Small means the world of a butterfly like a little lamb looking for cartoon butterflies.

The book in your hand wants to tell you powerfully to never and never be afraid of change. You may lose good things, but instead you will gain better things. This is what I guarantee, **Fidan**."

It was now making more sense to me and at once I was no longer sad or restless. I was finally listening to her fully and as she talked, I thought about all the times when I'd been a better version of myself.

"When you sow a seed under the soil, you no longer have that seed in your hand, right, **Fidan**? Because you buried it in the ground. That's what you should do."

"I don't think I can," I stumbled for words to say.

She reached forward and grabbed my hands in a delicate show of authority. "Listen to me, **Fidan**," she said, vehemently, as if she was certain that just a little bit of force could make me understand. "Do not doubt whether to check whether it is still there or not because you know you have to give him water, give him fertilizer, give him sun, so that he can come out and give you another thousand."

I nodded. She said, "So wait and have faith. Yes, it is faith. Believe in the decision you made! This means respect for yourself! There were things on that table at that moment that you had decided to do at that moment. So respect the intellect and the circumstances of your moment. And stop blaming yourself. This book wants to tell you why you should not get involved." I clutched the book to my chest and took a deep breath.

She let go of my hand. "Let me tell you something, Fidan. I think you deserve so much more than you're letting yourself have."

"It's tiring, I know," I said to her, refusing myself to cry. "I told you before," she said. "You are suffering from an emotionally unstable personality disorder which is why you're affected mostly by what happens around you and by people you do trust." "I am unstable," I said, close to tears. "And I hate how I don't feel good enough. I can't hold a conversation or keep my head up in a social gathering. I can't do anything. "Fidan you have to try just a little bit harder," May said. "When we reach the second half of life, we have to throw away useless things and keep life high in the balloon. Because life is declining and ending. One day you realize that there is no news ahead. And whatever it is, right now, is the presence of the moment. Reconciliation and acceptance of the moment." "Let me give you a piece of advice, Fidan," she said. "If you cook, cook right away, not in the future. Aging is a good thing, yes. The slower man is not farther away. You have to take care of what it is. The biggest truth in the world: nothing remains, and everything passes. Then it's all over. Fall in love in your old age, you have a much better mood now."

On the way home, I thought about all that she had said and I knew that it was I who would need to take a leap no matter how suffocating it would be to me. I called my sister again and waited as I had done nights before for her to pick. She did not. It was almost evening that a message popped into my phone. I read the message before looking at the sender and when I did, I felt a wicked surge of adrenaline pumping through my veins. I was angry but more than that, I felt as though I had been deprived of air.

The message was short and yet intense. It was from Adam and all he wanted me to know was that he missed me and wanted me back. It was a plea but I was not ready to understand the intricate lines which followed his message. We hadn't seen in years and now, suddenly, he missed me? That was unlikely. Yet when I showered and ate dinner, it was him and the message that crossed my mind, lingering with each breath of air I took. I did not reply the message even though a part of me had wanted to. Instead, I let it go, burying it amongst the pile of things I hated and things I couldn't care less about. Because, in truth, I couldn't care less if suddenly nostalgia hit him and he wanted me back. Nostalgia, as I had learned in a past life, was a step towards dependency and I didn't want that. All my life I had been saddled with the aching need to be with someone who could love me and want me in the same way they would the sun. In that, I became a subject of both ridicule and halved love. I became dependent on the men so that they could use me to the point where exhuastion mirrored my soul. I couldn't take it anymore. With Adam I had envisioned a world full of real love and devotion. Moving away from all that I had known in **Turkey** and trying to make Canada my new home had taken things away from me. Sure, I had hoped to start afresh but then I had learned how hard it was for me being a middle Eastern woman with a heavy accent. I learned I needed to really start over again, leveling the racist jokes and the frantic laughter of foreign friends.

The first time I had seen and come to learn about the new country was the culture shock. All the people and the way they lived, the way they existence in their bodies and outside of it, caged me in and I looked on helplessly. I would soon come to know that in leaving, I also had lost a lot.

It was the inevitability of traveling and leaving behind friends and family and my lover. The idea of friendship had not really come to me in the giving of things. Because I had not known a friendship so deep to be called anything beautiful, I did not know I had friends or could make friends. For me, they existed as individuals and strangers, unreachable and deadly. My family were not much to consider either. If it had been strictly my father with his stumbling words and crooked knees, I would have given up and cut all ties with him and the country of my birth. But there was my mother and my sister and both of those women had ripped my heart and sewn it back together effortlessly. Nostalgia was the one thing I often resisted. I couldn't afford to miss the past and the strangers. I couldn't afford to miss home when I had a place to stay right here. Adam therefore deserved nothing.

At work, I stacked the books on religion on the upper shelve and found a book about cloud gazing lying about on a table. I picked it up the way I usually did and took it back to the second shelf. Susan Fallings, the one woman at the book shop I actually got along with, came to meet me by the shelf. She folded her arms across her chest and gave a half smile. I could tell that she wanted to discuss something or say anything but I did not want to indulge in a conversation. It wasn't about her, though. It was strictly about me and everything I was feeling, stuck in the world where I was lonelier than ever and lost too. It was provably the main reason I was paying so much from my savings to see May, my therapist. She would help me, I know. "So..." Susan said, leaning forward. "What happened yesterday? You didn't come to work or call. I had to step in for you."

My bad. I should have called. "I'm sorry, Su," I said. "I really should have called. I hope it wasn't too hectic."

She shuffled her feet. "Oh it was the usual. Nothing too busy, that sort of thing." I nodded. "What happened though?" she asked.

I could tell that I had piqued her curiosity. It was the thing with Susan Fallings. She was always keen on learning and knowing and understanding that sometimes it came gratingly and I would pull back to catch a breath. I did not think I owed her much but the very idea of keeping her mute did not settle too well even for me. "I was a bit sick," I said to her. It wasn't a full on lie, regardless. Part of it was true. The part where I had gotten the message from Adam had made me feel painfully fragile and I had lost my voice and will and understanding of things. So it was also true that I had gotten a bit sick too.

She looked at me with concern. "I'm so sorry, Fidan. I didn't know, I would have come over." I didn't think we were past the work mate stuff or the endless chatter on books and fiction characters but as she looked at me keenly with concern, I threw away that thought. Perhaps we could truly be friends. I remembered my therapist, May, and the things she would constantly tell me and I held on to it now as I watched Susan in a new light. As we stood there, our sides held against the shelves stacked neatly with books on the cosmos and astrology, I saw that she was different and that we could grow into a friendship, real friendship, that would pull me out of the misery which I now was faced with. "It's fine, Susan," I said to her. "It was my fault; I should have called." "But how are you now? Do you need to get off work? I could stand in for you, you know."

I wanted to leave and take a stroll around the streets and inhale the smell of the sun before going home. I wanted to get away from all the books and human contact and race to my kitchen and make pancakes. Still I couldn't lay it all on her. She made me reconsider all of the things I had always known back in Istanbul and even here in Toronto. Now that I had my heart and mind open I could see clearly into these small actions and mold my thoughts with it to help myself grow and Lord knows I want to grow. "Thank you but I think I'd rather stay today," I said to her.

She squeezed my hand gently and moved away and I resumed putting the books back in their place. When a couple walked in, I met them by the door and offered up a smile that was almost real. The woman wanted a romance book but the man was more keen on a self-help book. I made a joke about him contradicting her in public and the woman laughed and threw her head back. I had never actually considered that to be something that could happen to me in my lifetime but making someone truly laugh gave me a type of euphoria that I never knew existed. I showed her to the shelf filled with romance novels and she picked three. He did not end up buying the self-help book and I reckoned it hadn't really been in his mind to get. At the door, she leaned over and she whispered,

"We really could be friends." I never knew it could feel that way but love was there and it felt alright. I told my therapist this when we met again a week later.

She offered tea immediatly and we sat and we had sandwiches first."Do you always offer your clients food first?" I asked her. She chuckled. "One can hardly classify this as real food, **Fidan**." "Still," I sipped from my cup. "It's food and it's delicious." She shrugged. "Let's simply call this our little scret," she said. "Just you and I, right?""Right!"

Sometimes, such as now, May became a friend and not just a therapist. However, on our first few minutes, the relationship had been strictly client and therapist. She was a good woman. She was a good person. "Do you like animals?" she asked suddenly. "Like pets?" She nodded. "Oh...I guess I do like them. Perhaps dogs? They are cute." "I have a dog named Eugene," she said and she laughed and I honestly could not trace the relationship between my situation and my love or dislike for pets. "It's a pretty name, I guess," I said. We were done with the meal. A secretary came in and cleared the table and May stood and walked to the window. The fan above was making the same noise again but, now, it was relaxing. I took off my shoes and curled up on the couch. The place smelt of her and a hint of a man's perfume.

"I think that I'm making progress," I whispered after a while of silence. She turned to meet my eyes. There was an unfamiliarity in those deep blue eyes and I stared hard until I was forced to look away. She did not look like my therapist. Instead she looked other-worldly, like a ghost of a past life I never knew existed. "What?" she asked. She folded her arms against her chest. I hesitated. Perhaps I was not making progress after all. "I don't know, May." She nodded and came to sit on her favorite chair. Her notepad and pen were on the the table still but she did not look like she wanted to write about me or anything else for that matter. I felt fear soaking into my bones; fear that she would begin to take and take like all the other men who had been in my life and I lost it. "I feel like this—all this talking and staring—is bullshit and I want to go home and be done with this," I blurted out. She did not look surprised and I did not regret it immediately. She ran a hand through her hair and offered a tight smile. "And what are you going to do at home, Fidan?"

"That's none of your business."

I wasn't the one talking even though the words were seemingly coming from my mouth and it bothered me. She arched an eyebrow. "You came here because you wanted help. You wanted a chance at life again, knowing that your childhood and young adulthood had birthed something sinister inside of you and you wanted to free yourself." I said nothing. "You are an impulsive woman, Fidan," she announced as if I hadn't already known. "But you can't keep hiding away behind curtains and veils and blaming everyone but yourself."

"I'm—I am sorry."

She reached over and she patted my arms. "It's going to be alright, **Fidan**. I promise you that it's all going to work out soon."

"Thank you," I said to her.

The silence was gentle afterward, not forced or awkward, just gentle. We did not stare at each other. I, for one, glanced at the rug and her pretty feet hidden away in a shoe. She was looking at the curtains and the woman on the portrait hung on the wall. There was no resemblance whatsoever but sometimes I wondered if the woman was May or a sister or a lover or a mother. I didn't ask her because I knew that they were a number of things I could not say and lines I should never cross.

I closed my eyes for a second and took a deep breath. There were things I now needed to know. "What usually causes you to show impulsive behavior?" May suddenly asked. I looked at her and we made a fleeting eye contact. "Be honest, **Fidan**," she said thoughtfully. "What makes you become impulsive?" I did not have to think. I already knew. "When I feel that someone is ignoring me, I act impulsively." "Just that?" She leaned closer, keen on my answers as if they were an unveiling of everything she hadn't already known. "Why did you act on impulse when you had been with Aboozar?" I frowned. We hadn't yet gone deeper in the conversations about him and now here she was asking me these questions. Didn't she know I was a lost woman? "I act impulsively when a man ignores me or when I feel like he's disrespecting me. Either he wants

to or he is betraying me. Or he is abusing me."
"Did he do all that to you?"

In truth, Aboozar had done none of that but I had left before he did. That was the truth, the only fact.

"I was made to believe that those kinds of love are non-existent..."

"Who taught you that?"

I couldn't tell. I told her so.

"But you do know," she said. "Think deeper, Fidan. You do know why you became like this! Tell yourself why and believe it because that is the truth."

After a while, I knew I had to tell her this. "Adam texted me, May." She arched an eyebrow. "What did he want?"

"He said he misses me and wants me back."

May touched her necklace and bit down against her lower lip. I watched her do that, perplexed as to why she was behaving as though it had somehow happened to her and not me. Then, later, her voice came back but it was bruised and I had to strain to hear her clearly. "Adam hurt you more than you realize, Fidan," she said. "Personally, I think he broke you in the way no one could. I won't spell things out for you because I'm simply here to guide you into going back to the right path. But you should know that Adam aided you into becoming... I interrupted her because I could tell she had a point and I knew it deep within my heart she was right.

I said, "Impulsive? Aggressive?" May nodded and gave me a pained smile. "Wait, observe, do not consider all behaviors as insults. Think deeply before saying anything, **Fidan.** Think before you react. Laugh more, cry less. Be bold. Take life by the throat and keep on walking with your head high up." "It isn't easy." "I know," she said. "Take a step first and the rest will follow." I did not go home immediately after the session. I took a walk as I had been hoping for. I inhaled the smell of early Spring seeping into my bones and thought about the book May had given to me and the things she would say. I had read only a few pages but it was enough to make me understand that I needed to be a better version of myself. I needed to pull myself out of the misery.

How many times had I said that to myself? I couldn't quite count but I knew, now, that I needed to make that work in every way I could. I took in the bittersweet smell of nature, marveling at how, looking at it clearly, I can see beauty in every little thing.

At home, in my new journal, I write about my impulsive state and how I needed to work through it.

I need to know the situations that could cause me to react immediately with harsh behavior. So when I recognize them, I prepare myself not to react quickly.

I also need to know the inner feelings that happen to me when I'm angry, that they start producing lava inside me like a volcano (like this when they come on because I recognize them, and I do not allow them to turn into impulsive behavior.

After I put the journal away, I walked into the kitchen and I made tea. The sun was still high up in the sky and across the kitchen sink, I could make out the constellations. It wasn't real, just some markings and lines that suddenly resembled the dizzy outlines of stars but it made sense to me. I leaned against the kitchen sink and stared at it, marveling at its audacity. Then the idea came to me to perhaps do some good to both myself and my loneliness because I had read somewhere that loneliness loved company. I took out my cellphone and I dialed her number. Susan picked up almost immediately which left me wondering if she hadn't been waiting for my call. That was stupid and crazy of course but still I wondered. "Are you okay?" she asked me and I could not tell what she was thinking at the moment. "Yes...of course I am," I said to her. It was pointless to beat around the bush. "Do you want to maybe come over? Perhaps for some tea and biscuits and book hangovers?" She laughed. It sounded intoxicating and I listened, hoping that there would be a day I would laugh as freely as this woman was. I could almost picture her in her kitchen like me or in her living room, phone pressed hard against her ears, her lips curled. I imagined her thinking, eyes sparkling with ease. "Are you serious right now?" She said this like I had just made a joke and she was not certain whether to laugh or be serious.

It was the truth: I had never made an offer this intimate before. She considered us friends, I could tell, but this was the first time I was desperate to invite her in. It showed in my voice when it cracked and broke and she did not laugh anymore. "Well...should I bring something?" she asked after a short while. "I don't think you should," I said to her. "I'll text you the address."

I sent her the address to my house before realizing I had done this with Autumn man. When he had sent me the address to his house, I had felt a little bit withdrawn from life and the complexity of living or the art of floating in love. I hadn't really known anything then because I had been young and naive and selfish. Autumn man did not truly know what love was but he easily could suck the air out of a woman. I stayed in the kitchen and put a pot on the stove. For a while I watched the orange and blue flames dance naked against the edge of the pot and I laughed like a maniac because there was no one around. I did not feel tied down to a person or a place or a distant memory. For once I did not feel confined to a certain space nor did anyone expect change from me. I was myself and even though this mirage would only last a few seconds, it did feel right. I poured water in the pot and then rice and when it began to boil and bubble, I turned the water out and put in a fresh one. It was to be a fact that perfect things were always subject to a certain kind of change. Nothing less than and that was it. When the rice was fully cooked, I made mint sauce along with it and went down to the storage room to get a bottle of white wine. I was already back in the kitchen when I saw her car pull up my driveway. She stepped down, closed all doors and came to the porch. I heard her ring the bell and then I walked and pulled the door open. She had a full smile and was wearing nothing but silly leggings and an oversized Tshirt. She was holding a small duffel bag and had a bottle of wine too. She hugged me fully, wrapping her arms over my body, joining both of us in a tight hold. Then she let me go and she glanced around.

"Oh my," she breathed. "You have a beautiful home." "Thank you," I said. It wasn't what I was expecting but I had to admit it sounded wonderful hearing it from her like that. "I brought wine," she announced. "I didn't know what else to bring, really."

I took it from her as well as her duffel bag. She adjusted her shirt and I smiled and said, "You look good for an all-nighter." She was smiling too. I was keen on a friendship with her, I wanted to. It had been a while since I invited anyone over and now that she was here, I was not certain what she expected. She said, "Your English is really good Fidan." "I learned it so I could move away from my hometown." She arched an eyebrow but she did not ask about the silly little details and I was more than thankful. She looked past my shoulder and inhaled deeply. "It sure smells delicious in here. Are you cooking or did you order something?" "Cooked," I said. "I'm totally bad when it comes to ordering. I always seem to flop."

She placed one hand on her chest and laughed and I saw that it reached her eyes. "Good God, Fidan. Why haven't we ever had this sort of conversation before?" I shrugged. But then it got me thinking. Why had we never been this close? Why had I always secluded myself from this kind of warmth? What had destroyed my desire or my reasoning? She was here regardless and that was all that mattered on the path of redemption. "I made rice, beef stew and mint sauce," I said. "Sounds lovely," she whispered. I showed her to my room and placed her bag on the bed. "Shower first and then come down. I'll set the table now," I said to her. She nodded.

Then I left her.

She was down thirty minutes later, her hair still wet, slowly and silently dripping into her oversized shirt. The shirt was worn and pale and stood in sharp contrast to her skin but it looked good on her. She seemed to be the only lady I had met who was capable of pulling this off and as much as I was fascinated by this, I let it pass. I had arranged the table so we sat and she helped herself to some beef. We did not talk. She chewed silently, her eyes deeply staring at the food on her plate. She was much younger than I was, of course, but I could tell we would be good friends if my heart and mind and soul would allow. She suddenly reminded me of my sister and the lingering sensation that I was being watched by someone or something. Then, Susan looked up at me and her expression softened. "I haven't tasted something this incredible. Thank you."

It was as though I had been reborn. Her choice of words lifted a weight I hadn't thought was within me and I laughed because it felt exhilarating. After eating, Susan offered to clear the table. I declined but she insisted so we each stood in the kitchen, our hands dipped in soapy water. The sun was orange in the sky now but just above the horizon, I thought I saw a faint splash of pink. It was quick and treacherous so that when I looked again, I discovered it had only been a figment of my imagination; that I would imagine something so distant and fragile and intense because of the freedom which this woman now offered me. "Are you...married?" Susan suddenly asked. I hesitated. She glanced at me sideways and then returned back to the dishes. "Don't overthink,

Fidan. I don't think it's important right now." She was overly matured in the way she handled things and in the words she said but since friendship was not something I was good at; I could not tell what she wanted me to do or how she wanted me to feel about her statement. I turned the words over in my head, uncertain, and cold and recklessly feeling as though I had been shoved hard against a brick wall. When we were done, we walked into the living room and together, we settled on the sofa. On the coffee table sat a book I hadn't known sat there still. Or perhaps I had known and had promised myself to burn or put away but had simply forgotten. She raised it up between us and read the title aloud. Then, she asked, "So... you are a fan of poetry? You don't look like..."

She stopped.

"It was a gift," I replied fast. It was a lie. Aboozar had bought it and sat down on the floor to read it aloud for both of us. The next morning, he had left the book there, on the floor, away from prying eyes and my insensitive mind. "I haven't read it though." She pulled the book open and she glanced at the first p age. "It's written by Aboozar Q," she announced as if I did not know that, as if I did not know how broken poetry was when it was stained by the lingering touches of a past lover. "I don't know who he is but then I think this will be good." It was better than good but I did not tell her that. She did not need to know how miserable this memory was making me feel.

"Do you want me to read it aloud?" she asked.

I could not tell no so I nodded and leaned back, afraid the book would break my resolve. She flipped to the middle and held the book closer. Here it goes, she said and began to read:

When her hands come to touch mine in the middle of the night,
I think about the birds in the sky and the grasses in an open field,
How fragile they are and yet how strong, how beautiful.
Ask me what love is and I'll whisper her name ten thousand times
Brush your lips on mine, my love, and I'll come home to you.

Then she stopped and she sighed. We did not talk about it for a while. Her phone began to ring and she excused herself. She stepped away from the living room to take the call. I did not mean to eavesdrop but then, later, I heard her arguing. She came back later and she put the book down on the table.

"My fiance," she said even though I did not ask. My guess was that my face betrayed me and she saw that I was interested, sort of. "Sometimes I hate him. Other times I can't stand the thought of leaving him."

I nodded. "Have you ever experienced this?" She waved her hand in front of her to explain better so I would know she was talking about love and relationships. They were the things I already knew. "Not wanting to love a person but finding yourself invested in them all the same? Like do you know how that feels like?"

I bit down against my lower lip until I could taste the blood of every kiss I had shared and every lie I had printed out of my lips. Then, I replied," I guess I have but it was a long time ago."

She said, "I don't know what to do, Fidan."

I gave her the advice my therapist, May, had given to me on our first session. "Do what's right, Susan, and everything will be fine."

"I dont know anything," she said. "Except that I love and hate him at the same time."

I sighed. "Well it happens to the best of us."

Later, we walked into my room and I closed the door. She did not take off her socks when she climbed in. I climbed in too beside her and we grabbed the sheets and pushed it closer to our bodies.

She breathed deeply. "You are withdrawn," she whispered. "I have watched you and know that often you tend to withdraw from things...and people." I shifted to look at her and curled my feet. "Was that why you had hesitated when I asked you to come over today? I sensed it when I asked, Susan."

"Yes," she said and chuckled nervously. "I was shocked, sorry."

"No, no don't apologise," I said because I knew that I had not been the most open person at work. I admit to keeping to myself and detailing my entire existence not to a person but to a book, my journal. "Thank you for coming today, Su. I needed the company, honestly."

She patted my hands and we locked eyes. It was not an attraction like how, often, I would feel attracted to a man but would keep my distance because I knew that I was emotionally unstable thanks to Autumn man and Adam who had sufficiently wrecked me and left me open and bleeding and cold. What passed between us was intimate like the bond of sisterhood and I wanted to thank her over and over again for making me feel a little bit powerful in her quiet words. "We should do this often," she said. "Personally I too would like the company." "To be with a bore?" She laughed and she dropped her hands and we turned to stare at the ceiling and the twirling fan. It reminded me of May's office and the pale walls painted a cold blue. It reminded of her hands twirling her favorite pen and the sudden keeness in her eyes when I said something she could not quite let go of. "Well maybe two boring people can make a right," she said in between laughter. Under the sheets, I joined hands with her and we stayed like that, pressed against the mattress with heaven in front of us. Behind me was the past; of memories like ghosts revolving around every little thing I did or every word I spoke. I did not feel particularly free or tall as I lay there with her but I felt a certain nostalgia when her low snores came to meet me and her hands dropped away from mine.

I saw my sister, small, open by the bed and I swallowed and touched her face. She was pale. I had almost drowned her. "I'm sorry, I'm sorry," I whispered to her. She said nothing but she was alive. She looked at me with those big brown eyes and I knew that one day she would hate me and we would break away, following different paths, never meeting. I opened my eyes suddenly. I had simply been dreaming. Susan was still here and she was fast asleep. I pulled the sheets away from my body and climbed out of bed. In the bathroom, I looked at my reflection in the mirror, wondering if I would see the woman who could not be happy hidden behind my eyes. She was there, a smile perched on her face, her lips bruised. She looked so much like me I could not tell what differentiated my body from hers. I could see the faint outline of wrinkles on my face but I did not let it cross my mind or longer endlessly. I was growing and that was it. I shook my head and the woman disappeared or perhaps she was lurking behind my teeth, sharpened by all the words I had said to hurt and the words I had kept, tucked away neatly in cages. For a second I could not breath. I could only see and what I saw was not lovely. When I walked back into the room, Susan was awake. "Can't sleep?" I sniffed. "I just went to the bathroom." She pulled the sheets tighter. "Don't think too much about what you might consider to be your flaws. Tomorrow you'll be significantly better and the day after, you'll live." I sniffed and wrapped myself closer. "Thank you, Susan. I needed that." She nodded and closed her eyes. I sat down on the edge of the bed and sighed deeply. Later I wrote down a few key points on my journal after she had fallen asleep again and I was alive for the first time in weeks. I was going to show my therapist. I could picture her now, relaxed. She would call this progress in the same way I was calling it now. But I wrote the words in italics so it would stand out from all the pages I'd scribbled my heart ache in.

- Let the hard days make you a better person
- Dream big, work hard and stay focused
- Do not depend on anyone in life and do not cling to anyone!

At the next session, I sat down on the floor instead of the couch. May glanced through the journal. It was supposed to be a secret between the journal and I but I had made a lot of progress since the last session and I needed to get her opinion on the changes I was making for myself. I told her about Susan and what she had said to me and May smiled and wrote it down in her notepad. Then I told her about how the weight I had felt for the longest time now seemed like a shadow of a past life. "That's...really good, Fidan," she said breathlessly and I thought she too had been running for far too long. "I know it is," I said to her. She ran a hand through her hair. "Keep doing this —all that you've written down — and I'm certain it will all work out. This makes me happy more than anything else.

When she asked me if I wanted tea or coffee, I thought about hugging her. And when the tray of tea and biscuits was rolled in, I hugged her. She seemed taken aback, as if it was mostly rare for a patient to take her in their arms. We did not talk. Then her hands came behind me and she held me just as I held her. We did not talk. Later, I was the one who tiptoed to the window. I could feel her gaze piercing from behind me but, for once, I felt reborn. "The woman in the picture, who is she?" I asked her sometime later. She shook her head and then she hesitated. I believed she was playing the words in her head, her response and the truth. Somehow when her lips pursed and her eyes wavered, I knew she was about to tell me. Two full minutes had passed. The whirring of the fan would not stop and surprisingly, I did not want it to stop. "My sister," she said. "She died years ago but I still think of her in the present." —I nodded. "Must be why you kept insisting I called my sister and talked to my mother, right?" May chuckled. —"You never truly know the time you have left, yeah." I placed one hand against my chest in surrender. —"I really should call again then. Try a bit harder to reach home." She nodded. "It's always a bit of trick, really, to feel that connection again with them but I suppose trying is not such a bad thing."

"Then I will call them," I said.

Then I walked back to sit on the couch. She was twirling her pen, biting her lower lip and I could tell she was thinking.

"What about Aboozar?" She suddenly asked. I paused, uncertain. Had she asked the question as a form of trickery? Had I heard the name fall from her lips simply as a figment of my imagination? I could not tell for certain so I remained mute. May leaned closer. She suddenly looked older. "I've seen how you have made progress with yourself and the people you've found along your path. For example, Susan and me and the strangers you've met in the street." I was listening hard to what she had to say even though I could not understand a single word she was saying.

"For you to fully find yourself, Fidan, you should call him and you should talk to him." I shook my head. "No, I can't." —"Why?" I shrugged. "It's been years, Fidan. Both of you need to have this talk. Find some closure. Be brave about this." "But I couldn't possibly..." I stopped myself and glanced down at my feet. "Would that help?" "I believe so." At work, I walked to meet Susan down at isle two. She was done arranging the books but she still had one in her hands. When she saw me she waved as if we were not simply inches away from each other. "Thank you for the other night," she said. "It was wonderful."— "I'm just glad you could make it." Something glistened in her fingers. A silver ring, something I had not noticed when she came to the house. She saw me staring and she smiled shyly. She said, "He asked me to marry him. Poor bastard!" We both shared a laughter that later made me realize I was lonely and needed closure. —"Well... congratulations, Susan." She kissed my cheeks and when I turned away, I knew it was time to call him. At home in the evening, I sat down on the floor in the kitchen as the moon came in, halved through the curtains. The stars were few in the sky but I simply did not care. I took my phone, dialed his number and waited. In the waiting, I thought about all the times we had shared and the daring moments when his hands had given me both comfort and relief. I needed all that now. I wanted closure and a chance to be free. His voice came on suddenly and he took my breath away.

"Hello, Fidan."

CHAPTER FIVE
Reborn

I wrapped the shawl around my neck and combed my hair with the tip of my fingers. The sun had come into the house now, stretching its hands like tendrils over the walls, masquerading in the colors flushing both the walls and the floor. I stood there, by the door, and stared at the things I could see and feel and touch. Everything looked spectacular. It wasn't for the fact that things had changed or that I had replaced half of the things which now occupied the space. No, it would come to be more than that. It was an irreplaceable feeling; vignettes only I could see. Slowly a lump began to form in my throat and I thought, for a while, I was going to cry. I thought that I would begin to slowly burn and tearfully pull away because of this permanence of good things. I could tell that things were about to change. I unlocked the door and stepped out into the chilly air. Although the sun was high up, I could feel a cold envelop me. This time it was a welcome touch and I clung unto the fault that I could somehow be happy.

My car sat silently by the corner but I had made up my mind that I was going to walk. It was a Sunday and just over the trees and cars and the moving clouds, I could make out the faint sounds of church bells. I had never truly been one with the religion because my ma had taught us something different and I had grown up with different ideas and values. This time around though, I did not feel fear that like if I listened to the church bells I wouldn't fall on my knees. It came to me then, that it did not matter if I fell on my knees or if I simply kept walking. What mattered, infinitely, was the good in my heart and the lucidity I now felt.

My skin no longer felt like daggers, placed steely over my frame. It became to me some sort of guidance, a beautiful flaw that made me Fidan. Therapy had worked and helped me to see things differently and now I had friends who knew me in the ways that formed the existence of things. I stepped on maple leaf and when I heard the crunching sound, I thought about my mother and my sister and my lost country; how I wanted to go back and hug them and stare into the vacancy, guiding my emotions back to my skin. I had not called them yet but sometimes I wished it was simple. It really wasn't. Because what would I say to both of them? The country and the men I had been with had shoved reality down my spine in fistfuls and it had taken a toll on me and my body, soul and mind. So what could I say to them that would mean something worthwhile? Still, now that I knew I had been broken by the men that had found their way into my life, I wanted to change everything. I wanted to grow and build myself from the scratch and learn to love myself again. I loved the country and the soft smell of apple juice and morning coffee and the fleeting eyes of strangers waving at me. Now, I had found peace and contentment in the small details because I believe that it was those small deals that made me feel like a woman again. There were some things I particularly loved most. Like how, sometimes, I would ride my bicycle around the street with my hair flipping behind me and I would see the little children waving and kicking their legs. It would be winter again. We all knew that seasons change and so did humans. I enjoyed sipping on my tea while looking at snow drops in winter. Here, I could think before making decisions and contemplate on the things that needed believing in. I could dip my hands in water and feel freedom surging in my veins. Here, I had finally learned to love myself and appreciate the life I have.

As I walked, I inhaled the fresh morning breeze and took in the sun like it was a part of me and I had invariably become a part of it as well. Canada and I hold each other so tight because we both understand the growth and how long it would take to cross the stars. I found him already seated outside under the blue awning. For a moment I stood there, behind him, wondering if perhaps I should turn back and run. I could thank caprice for this indecisive moment. I had sent him the text and he had invited me here, to the place where we'd first met. Now, here, I could not tell what I wanted most. This was the deciding moment. Here. I could either turn around and go back and grow alone, side by side with nature or I could sit with him and learn to love again.

I sighed. Then I knew it was time. I took a step forward and then another until I was face to face with him. I did not call out his name. I simply mouthed it, afraid that if I curved my lips around his name, it would turn to hate. He started to get up but I stopped him with a wave of the hand. Aboozar settled back on his chair and placed both hands on the table. A waitress with a lovely smile came forward and I asked for an apple juice and a cheese cake. "You haven't changed," he said to me.

I gave him a tight and awkward smile and listened as he said his order. When the waitress was gone, he leaned in and I could both smell and taste him. How my tongue missed his and my body, his hands! "You look stunning," he said. I was well aware I was older and he was too and we both had wrinkling stripes on our skins in subtle forms but it wasn't what I was worried about. I did not know how to talk or react now that he was before me. I knew that if I let it remain like this, it would become awkward and he would leave. Now that I was here with him, I did not want him to leave. I wanted both of us to stay. "You haven't changed a bit." I said to him. He chuckled and looked around. Then when his eyes found mine, I wanted to fall back into him and kiss him. "Well you'll find that I've changed considerably." "Physically?" He smiled. "In every way, Fidan." Our orders were brought along with a smile that stretched heavenly until I began to fear it would break. Her name tag read Jessy and so when I thanked her, I said her name, firmly, softly as though we'd been friends already. "Enjoy," she announced before walking away. When the waitress was gone again, I sipped my orange juice and watched Aboozar with his tall glass of cold coffee. "Do you still smoke then?" I asked Aboozar. He frowned but it was gone the next moment, so fleeting I could have mistaken it for anything else. He said, "I don't smoke anymore, Fidan. Is that a good enough change?" I laughed and cut a piece of the cake with the edge of the fork. I was perfectly aware that he was watching my every move and that he was seeing me again for the first time in years after our fight and the heartbreak. The emotions were coming back again, I knew, and yet I could not resist it because I too wanted it. It's a good change," I replied and chewed on the piece of cake. —A couple holding hands walked by and I turned to Aboozar. "How are you?" He shrugged. Then I leaned back and knitted my fingers together. "I used to wonder about you, you know. I used to wonder how you were and if you still wrote about the things you loved." "And yet you didn't call," he muttered beneath his breath. "You can hardly blame me, Aboozar," I said. Was I letting the terrible emotions rise again to the surface? I didn't want that. I wanted to break away from that burden. "What was I to do learning you were with a wife?" He hesitated. "We were estranged, Fidan. I was going to divorce her." "You should have told me before we both fell in love with each other." Aboozar sipped from his cup again, placed it down and nodded. He looked right past my shoulders and grunted. "I should have told you," he said. "But I guess I was scared of you leaving." "I did leave," I said. He laughed but I could tell that there was some measure of pain laced in that simple laughter. It was mesmerizing to watch, knowing that one of us had lied and the other had acted impulsively. He said, "Well isn't that ironic then?" I cut another piece of the cake and chewed quietly. The silence was slowly becoming awkward but none of us were willing to break it. It would stretch and stretch over this walls and the hushed conversations of strangers and the people passing by and the sun. It would meet the sun and color it dark until we lost our footing and then we would fall. Aboozar sighed. "Thank you for calling, Fidan. I mean I always wanted to call but I was certain you'd moved on." "Haven't you?" I asked him. He looked at me for a moment and then away at his cup. "I tried to. It's been years right? I should have moved on but I could not. It isn't easy to let go of someone, Fidan." "I know that all too well," I said to him. "But I'm growing and that is what matters: growth." "So... you've moved on?" He leaned closer and he took my hand in his. "If you've moved on, Fidan, why did you call me?" —"Because I haven't!" Slowly Aboozar let me go and he nodded. "That's a relief." I licked my lower lip, turning the prospect in my head. Did I really want this man back? I still loved him, that much was certain and although we had gone through a bit of turbulence, we were here and we were fine and we would be for a long time to come. "I could never let you go, Aboozar," I whispered. "Do you think we could...try again perhaps?"

He blinked twice and ran a hand through his hair. "I want to be honest with you from now on. I want you, Fidan. I want to try again but this time, rid-

ding myself of the flaws which had made you leave."
The promise was gentle and it touched me considerably. I offered to pay for both of us but this man refused.
"I just want to." he said, standing. —"Always have
been a gentleman, I suppose," I said with a shy smile.

He came back and he took my hand and I was
once again reminded of the past years and how his
hands and mine had grown accustomed to each
other. The tingling sensation came again, blooming like a carnivorous plant, eating out all the self
doubt and fear and anger. It was all over now. Walk
with me, Fidan." he said and he pulled me along.

We held hands as we walked down the street. My shoes
hit the concrete with a low thud, matching his rhythm
as though it was always meant to be like this; as if, regardless of every turbulence felt between us and against
the universe, we were again here, happy and healthy.

He showed me the clouds as they moved steadily in
the sky. Then he showed me his heart in his hands,
holding it out for me to see how fragile it had become over the years. Aboozar handed his heart to
me with both hands, afraid it would fall and break
all over and again. It was old and worn out but it was
as beautiful as it was the day he told me he loved me.
We were standing beneath an oak tree when he placed
his heart in my hands. The wind threw a vortex of
grasses our way and the birds sang off key. Still, it was
the most beautiful sound I had ever heard.

He leaned closer, pining me against the tree. It was
not a rough move but it made me feel a bit afraid. He

was quick to notice and he pulled back softly. He was apologizing before I even had the chance to stop him.

"I'm sorry, Fidan," he said.

I took hold of his hand again and brought it to my lips. I kissed his fingers one at a time, completely enthralled by his hands and body and manners. It was true: he had lied to me years before and that lie had caused us to break away from each other. But we were here now, together and he loved me and I loved him just as much.

"Be with me," he muttered underneath his breath. I let him kiss my lips and wrap me in his hands. "Of course, Aboozar," I said to him.

We walked over to my place and we sat down on the couch and he read for me, a poem he'd written.

I have lost myself, find me in you
Sit in my eyes, watch your glory
Let the black waves of your hair be in my hands
Let my head rest on your shoulder
Cypress is not a mirror of power
Watch your beauty in my poem!

And it felt just right.

F
— ✕ —
M